WEDDINGS AND FUNERALS

WEDDINGS AND FUNERALS

Sara Maitland ● Aileen La Tourette

BRILLIANCE BOOKS

Published by Brilliance Books 1984
Copyright © Sara Maitland and
Aileen La Tourette
1984

ISBN 0 946189 01 3 (hardback)
ISBN 0 946189 06 4 (paperback)

BRILLIANCE BOOKS
14 CLERKENWELL GREEN   LONDON
EC1

Printed and bound in Great Britain by
Nene Litho and Woolnough Bookbinding,
both of Wellingborough, Northants

Typset by MC Typset, Chatham, Kent

CONTENTS

THE WEDDING STORIES

THE SIN STORIES

THE MADNESS STORIES

THE BIRTH STORIES

THE FUNERAL STORIES

THE WEDDING STORIES

The Triangular Eye: 1

I would be premenstrual on my wedding day.
You would, echo her sisters, the bridesmaids, in the mirror.
  'I could be pregnant,' she says aloud.
  'So could I,' they giggle, each in her turn.
  'Yes. But for you it would mean something different.'
  'A trip to the Marie Stopes,' one says crudely.
  'I mean,' she says with dignity, taking up her hairbrush,
'it would mean terror and change. For me it would mean
routine and predictability. That's why I'm not.'
  'That's why we're not, too,' they give it back to her, like
throwing the bridal bouquet back in her face, she feels. She
waves her hairbrush.
  'Get out of here, will you, please? I want to be alone.'
  Madam Butterfly, her mother, floats in, handsome in
crimson slashed with indigo. She palms a glass of champagne. Her palm is luckily cool and will not smear the chilled
glass.
  She sets it down.
  'She wants to be alone,' one of the sisters explains.
  'Do you know what Garbo did on her wedding day?'
another hesitates in the doorway to inquire.
  'Climbed out the window,' she nods in the mirror.

'Goodbye.'

'See you later, alligator,' another says affectionately.

She manages a crocodile smile.

Madame Butterfly mouths a kiss in the mirror and turns on her delicate heel.

'I'll leave you to your thoughts, darling,' she murmurs. She, too, turns around in the doorway. 'It's a good idea to have a quiet little moment before the onslaught,' she says, more or less to her own reflection. Her eyes flicker to the bride's. They hold for a second like duellists' eyes behind their masks. Then she's gone, the door softly closed behind her.

'Have you ever slammed a door in your life, Mother?' the bride asks in a stage whisper. 'Have I?'

Now, there's a question. She picks at a cuticle. Is it a sin to deprive the unconceived of life? If they're there in preconception, might they not have souls?

She leans towards the mirror. Madame Butterfly's mask was perfectly applied. A reproach to a face which is still just a face. Fingers reach for the little jar of foundation. Her fingers are hot. She curls them around the champagne glass to cool them, then lifts it to her lips.

In a minute she'll send a posse. It's too quiet, she'll think, as she thought when I was a child playing alone, absorbed and happy. Something had to interrupt such perfect concentration.

Funny, our species makes king butterflies of the women. The men are mourning doves today. What can come of the mating of a butterfly and a mourning dove? A poor ungainly bird with useless gauzy wings like a thalidomide child's arms.

Jesus *Christ*.

So she said, aged ten, confronted with a front-page story of thalidomide horrors, graphically illustrated, intended to shock, intended to sell the rag that had printed it.

Exploitation, she wrote, spelling the word out in her head.

Addressed it to The Editor and sent it off; but it wasn't really the crassness of the newspaper she was protesting against. It was the crassness of the cosmos in which such a thing could happen.

She raises her head and looks at herself.

Wonder when will it come? Roll on the red sea, not back. PMT means swarms of memories, associations and feelings, especially feelings. None of them specially welcome. It's like being shaken by the scruff of the neck, once a month. Knocks you awake. Like doing a round in the ring with an invisible opponent. Shadow-boxing. Like hearing the sharp sweet pipes of Pan in the forest at night. Derivation of panic. Like: panic.

'Don't panic,' she says to her reflection, rubbing in foundation. 'You can always – you can always . . .'

Get a divorce? Run away? Commit suicide?

Sleep.

But you won't sleep, or if you do you'll wake up once a month at least. There's the rub.

But I'm not planning to sleep.

Oh, no?

White dress like snow under which you'll grow numb, my dear.

Don't be stupid.

She takes out the compact with the blue enamel design on top, wedding present from MB. The necessary somethings blue and new. MB determined to make this work.

Snow blurs lines, blots out distinctions. Only while it falls, only while the veil hangs in the air, everyone a bride. Then it shapes and sharpens everything again, emphasizes singularly with shadows.

Blush.

Why do we like red cheeks? As if the colour rose from the heart.

From the heart! From the plastic case.

My heart is a blood-red sun. Who said that? No one, probably.

Red sky in the morning, sailors take warning.

I'm getting tired of my mind.

She slurps the rest of the champagne, deliberately piggish.

Pearls before swine, as she clasps them on.

The moon's doing, my mind. PMT. Dismiss it. Biology. Deny, deny. A perversion of truth. A distortion of reality. Once a month the veil lifts, and we shudder, to see the shadows.

Eyeshadow. More blue, on the lid. Borrowed from Kate. A plethora of blues, all shades, this a good healthy aquamarine, nothing brooding.

Eyeliner. Never got it close enough to the actual rim of the lid, not unless you worked at it.

She works at it.

Who am I so angry at? The moon?

Mascara wand. Black, mystic.

A soft tap at the door.

'Shall I help you with your veil, dear?' She's not leaving anything to chance.

'In a minute, Mummy.'

Don't overplay your hand.

There's ever so little time left to think of Paul.

There's all the time in the world to think of Paul. And why 'ever so'?

Because he says it. It's starting already. Buried in snowdrifts. It does blur, it does. Shadows are negatives. They name only types, they lose features, erase every distinguishing mark, every detail. And yet snowflakes are mortal, individual, like us, each one different. Like thumbprints. Used to identify the guilty.

But snowflakes? Used to whitewash.

I'm a negative. This is a guilty party, a festival of whitewash. Will there be whispers?

'You know she had that –'

'No. I didn't. Know she was like that.'

'She isn't now.'

Another soft tap at the door, as if she can read the drift of my thoughts. It's not a drift, it's a rip-tide to drag me away from here, it's a whirlpool to pull me down like a ballerina in quick pirouettes.

But I was down before. When I was pretending. The mask is set, but the eyes flicker in the mirror. They'll flicker behind the veil but no one will see.

Unless Jane comes.

MB doesn't know I sent her an invitation. Didn't put her on the list, of course. Anyway she won't come. She'd toss it into the bin, embossed paper and all. She'd heave it down the plughole. And love. And me.

She'd bury her love in the snow, keep me alive suspended in nitrogen whatever-it-is. Not snow, not for Jane: dry ice. The scorcher, the preserver.

Another tap, louder. Come along, please.

Paul, I must think of Paul.

For ever.

Tap-*tap*.

'Mother, I'll let you know when I'm ready.'

'All right, dear.'

Nose for rage like a pig for truffles.

Enough of that individual nonsense, time to be gathered and harvested, time to be snowed into your veil, walled into your eyes. Like an icon. They're all the same face. Huge sad eyes, but all the same eyes.

How about an icon with furious eyes? With red eyes from weeping too much wine changed to salt water? How about a madonna screaming?

Jane would love it! How about one sticking her tongue out? How about . . .

Jane.

The thought had come. The inspiration, to break the mould.

Now I can go through with it. Let the cock crow three times for me, now . . .

'Mother?'

Snowfall without flakes, every circle the same. She adjusts with cool fingers, then lifts the froth for a Judas kiss, cheek to cheek. She's in the lipstick generation.

She knows whose name is on my lips.

Down the stairs to the mounting music. Is it better or worse to be married at home? Not even home is safe. For better or for worse here I stand at the foot of the stairs, with a smiling man. A bouquet magically in my arms like a wind-borne baby.

Head cold and empty as a snowball under its double masks. Triple: two layers of veil and the make-up.

Oh moon, oh mother. The ritual might freeze but it might also thaw. Masks were once used for healing.

Yes, but they weren't pretty.

Goddess with perfect pitch, make this ring true.

Make me be utterly here, just this once. All present and accounted for. A quorum of my own contradictions so that I can make a valid decision.

'Candles look funny in daylight,' she sniffed. 'Not worth it.'

'If I close the curtains she'll wonder why.'

'I know what.' She took the quilt from my bed with one majestic heave. 'C'mon. You can blow them out, it's your birthday.'

I was ten. Everyone else had gone home. We filled our pockets with candles and scrambled upstairs as we're now scrambling down. She led me, with an inquiring look, into the seldom-used formal parlour. Cold, as they kept them in Irish families, for wakes. We didn't have wakes, but we still kept the parlour cold.

'No one comes in here, do they,' she whispered.

I shook my head.

She threw the blanket over the piano to make a tent and then we sat inside it with the candles. I'd brought a plant to stick them in the dirt. I couldn't think of anything else. She seemed to approve, smiling, with an arm around my shoulders.

'We'll get married,' she said confidently. 'When we're twelve.'

'How can we?'

'Oh, they let you get married younger if you marry a girl.'

'They do?'

'Of course they do!'

It must be another example of what my mother called Common Sense. I could never figure out what it was or how it worked. I was glad she knew. It made me feel good about marrying her.

'Know what they'll ask you tomorrow?'

'What?'

'How it feels to be ten. Isn't that a stupid question?' It is. And they got what they wanted: a stupid answer.

The Triangular Eye: 2

In some countries you can get off murder for PMT.

That's what I said to myself as I got ready. Plead insanity if you have to plead.

Then I thought, shit no. That and being a lesbian'll finish me. Life in some loony bin where the masks don't come off.

As I fitted the mask on.

What made me think of it? Old mythologies of healing. You imitate the thing you fear, or the thing you desire. Sympathetic magic. I could've gone dressed as a bride but I didn't fancy it.

So I went as a crone. I thought if I could take that shrivelled-up self and put her outside instead of carrying her around inside me like an ancient foetus grown old without delivery, maybe then I'd be delivered.

Guts, they said.

Nerve, they said.

Cheek, they said.

Sounds like an autopsy, I thought.

Of all the gall, someone said.

I liked that one best. It rhymed.

At first they thought I was a sidekick of the groom's pulling a practical joke. As they came out of the house towards the marquee on the lawn, I stationed myself at the entrance, the tent flap thing. I wanted to see her walk towards me in that get-up.

Then they thought I was some leftover girlfriend of his. That really annoyed me. I had to take care that they got the idea. But first I had to find a quiet place to scowl at them from, like Quasimodo from the belfry.

There was one woman alone. All the rest were couples, or sisters or brothers or cousins or something avuncular. Why isn't there a word like that for aunts? It just goes to show.

Just remembering it makes me grind my teeth like an old cranky lady. That seemed to me to be about the most objectionable thing I could do from behind a mask, apart from just being there.

There was even one person who was something or other once removed.

'Wish they'd remove him again,' I said to someone at my elbow who turned out to be a camera. Most sympathetic eye I'd seen all day. Objective. I'd tell her my story, as I'd come to play the Ancient Mariner. She was the woman alone.

'Let's sit down. I'm through for the moment.'

She didn't seem particularly fazed by my outfit, though she, too, had made the absurd assumption that I was something to do with him in the monkey suit. I quickly put her right, and she smiled.

One picture's worth a thousand words. She didn't have to tell me. Knowing we were comrades-in-arms gave me confidence. I plunged right in and told her all about Frances, first I told her not to judge by appearances, that she was no rent-a-bride. I should know. Told her the places we'd been together, till she decided I was a phase.

She kept getting up to take pictures and whenever she stood up I got a clear view of the High Table, or whatever they call it, with Frances in the middle like Lady Macbeth.

She couldn't see my face, behind the mask. With all that

make-up on I could hardly see hers.

'Maybe this is twisting her arm,' I defended myself to Evelyn, the photographer, as she sat down. 'But it hurts me more than it does her. It's an act of survival, not terrorism.'

'Maybe sometimes they're the same.'

I wasn't really listening. We painted ourselves once, all over, with flowers and faces and signs. Then we washed it all off and stayed in our colourful bath till the water got cold and we had to run for the bedroom. The sheets were left the shade of a bruise when it's starting to heal and it gets that bright yellow in it and looks worse than ever. I kept them.

'She says I'm not sentimental. She says I don't understand about things like this because I'm not fucking sentimental. Would I have done that? Kept it? Unwashed? Even slept on it sometimes? Actually, it's filthy now. Actually,' I had to confess, Evelyn looked so sympathetic I felt a fraud. 'It got so bad I had to let the dog sleep on it. Does that mean she's right?'

She smiled.

'Unsentimental people don't even have dogs,' I adjudicated for myself. 'So there. I wouldn't've given those sheets to any old dog anyway. Just this one. She slept with us, too, sometimes. So it seemed sort of appropriate.'

She nodded.

'What about you?'

'Parties are my religion,' she said with another smile like a flashbulb. 'I follow the crowd, in a literal sense.'

'But always stay a little bit apart,' I reminded her. Her face was better than you thought, at first. Frances wanted her face to rape, on impact. But this face kind of lights the lamps and waits.

'Weddings are my least favourite parties.'

'Mine too. Especially this one.'

We drank. I'm getting a wee bit maudlin on the champagne. Must do something, hit and run before I crumble.

'I was in two weddings as a child,' she said softly. 'I knew then I never wanted one of my own. It seemed wonderful to be a bride, but what then?'

'Anticlimax.'

She nodded. 'I never made any one of my own great state occasions,' she grinned. 'First Communion, got measles. Confirmation, mumps. Birthday parties, I was always about to get my period, so I was there but not, you know?'

'I know. I'm like that today.'

'Me too.' She grimaced. 'Weddings do it every time. And of course there was never any question of a wedding,' she made a dismissive gesture, 'once I knew. But even if I'd been straight I'm not sure I'd have had one. It's like preferring Easter to Christmas, because it's a moveable feast. It goes according to the moon.'

'Christmas goes according to the sun.'

'Yes, but the sun is fixed. I prefer moons.'

'I know.' I grinned at her as flirtatiously as I could. I could see Frances watching us, and her mask slipped just a little over one eye, enough to reveal a greenish flare. 'So do I.'

Eating smoked salmon behind the mask was a funny sensation. Almost intravenous. I was pigging away nervously when it occurred to me to ask myself why I was nervous. Hadn't I had my big moment by the flap of the tepee? Was there anything else for me to do, anything public and difficult, that is?

Are they the same? Evelyn asked. 'Public and difficult?'

'I can't very well make a small intimate gesture under these circumstances,' I snapped. She'd definitely struck a nerve. If I'd known her better I'd have inserted an 'of course' after that thought.

'You could try,' she said blandly, lighting a cigarette. 'I should think the only thing you have to fear –'

'Is fear itself?'

'Is the danger that she might think you only wanted revenge.'

'I do want revenge.'

'I was under the impression there was something else you wanted.'

'Yes, but I can't have that!'

'If you're that convinced, then you must've come here looking for revenge.'

I could've bashed her with her camera. As if she knew, she picked it up and started snapping away.

'Listen,' I said to her, as she came back to the table to reload. 'You know what?'

'What?'

'You're the terrorist, that's what. You try and steal their souls, don't you? Like the old superstition? Capture them?' I was pretty well loaded myself by then.

'I try to capture a moment in time,' she replied. 'That's all. Not to steal anything. People think that because they feel exposed. Or because they want to forget. But I don't believe in forgetting.'

'Neither do I.'

'Most people seem to feel pictures confirm them in some way. Their pictures or something. Rather than detract from them. It's seeing yourself on the other side of the mirror that's odd.'

'Like in somebody's eyes. Like love. But then when it's over – the moment – you have to lapse back into yourself again.'

'But that's part of the process. Like going back to the darkroom and developing them. You can't be with someone all the time. You have to go and develop your memories – or something. You have to sleep, for Christ's sake!' She laughed a rich champagne chuckle.

Frances was staring again.

'It's all part of the process,' she finished. 'My whole life is bound up with the process – and so is yours.'

'Different processes.'

'Maybe. Maybe just different methods.'

'I have an idea. If I ask her to dance, will you take pictures?'

'Join the methods.'

'Well?'

'Of course I will.'

'Better not wait.' I stand up on the two sticks I'd hobbled up in, to complete the part. They gave me a terrible feeling of frailty, as if I really needed them. The room seemed to hush slightly as I wobbled over towards Frances. With all that champagne inside me, I did need them.

'What the hell do you think you're doing,' she whispered furiously. 'Trying to humiliate me?'

Upstage her, did she mean? Evelyn was right, this could backfire. I could drop down on my knees in front of her but that'd be over the top.

'Frances,' I threw my sticks away in sheer bravado, as if I anticipated acceptance. I anticipated having to play pick-up-sticks in about a minute. 'Would you like to dance?'

She looked at me hard. I'd have taken off the mask but I sensed she wanted it left on, for effect. So I just held her eyes through the mask, and she held mine through hers.

Then she stood up, and held out her hand.

The Triangular Eye: 3

Back to the darkroom. Home!

My rabbit hutch. Not cramped, though; room to stretch. I stretch. Every movement in here makes you aware of the walls, not crowding you, just there. I never feel lost in here.

Deep breath. My favourite perfume; sharp, chemical. A constant rain of fluids keeps the air rinsed and fresh, despite the haze from my cigarettes. There's a strong whiff of coffee in the blend, too.

This room used to be a larder. The door leads to the main house through the kitchen. I commute from here to the coffee pot, hardly noticing my to-ings and fro-ings.

There's a bottle of Scotch strategically placed on a shelf. If I've worked a good solid day, I have a whisky and soda at five. Used to make it six, but I'd waste the last hour fretting and fumbling. Funny how hard it was to trust my own sense of time enough to move the drinking hour forward. Felt like the first step down the path towards having a splash of Scotch on waking; but it wasn't, of course. Why do I still have that stubborn idea of linear progressions when everything tells me it doesn't work like that? I set my own pace, my own discipline. I'm ready at five. I emerge at five.

Occasionally, if I'm going out in the evening, I make it a

little earlier or a little later. I never skip my ceremony of re-entry into the world. If I do I arrive undeveloped, still in the negative stage. Living alone, working alone, you need your rituals no less than couples or families do, to negotiate the crossing from inner to outer. You have to build your bridges.

I hear voices and motors distantly, as if across water. Sometimes I listen for minutes at a time, crouched over on my stool or standing, transfixed, without a thought in my head. My process in the darkroom is silent. I love the silence, and I am grateful for the sounds.

Today I want to get on with it. It's been a week since the wedding. As I close myself in with my steaming mug of coffee and light a cigarette, I'm aware of an uncomfortable feeling I've fended off for that week. It's hard to fend things off in here. Bit of a confessional. I was afraid to develop these pictures before, afraid I'd be jealous.

That's better. Now it's out of the bag and I can see its green cat's eyes gleaming in the dark. A big cat, a tiger. I've seen it before. You see a lot of things, in the dark; but only what you bring in with you.

My tiger's the photo of a dream, developed over some ten years. Successive dreams, successive negatives dipped in some nameless fluid to become a memory. I always wake up richer from the dream.

A woman sits at an easel, in the middle of a marsh. The clouds are dark but the sun is shining. Cat tails rise around her. The pools of water are gold on the marsh, from the sun. She wears a black dress with gold buttons and a black turban. Shadows are black, reflections gold; they thatch the spongy ground.

She's painting a tiger. The picture is extremely clear, like a photograph. The sun behind her acts as a sort of lens; the dark clouds help develop the picture. Sometimes the woman falls asleep in the sun, and the tiger springs down from the easel to circle her, faster and faster, a ring of fire or gold wedding band to warm and protect her. Sometimes the tiger stalks off across the marsh, light as a bird, dipping his head to sip from the golden pools. He's always back on the paper when she wakes up.

I sleep in here sometimes, fitfully. Awake, I never see the woman, only the tiger. She's too much me to need seeing. Her age changes. Sometimes she's very old, sometimes a child. The tiger's age is constant.

Today there's a green glow of envy in his face, a certain sulky cast to his posture. What is it, my beauty? Proud and sleek, but a little fantastic, and always alone?

Yes, my sullen familiar, you are the golden stranger at the feast. Usually you have no appetite for what's served up along with the canapés. You purr like a motor travelling between their clusters, refreshed by the shutter's click against the blurred murmur of voices, the prevaricating laughter.

But not this time. Oh, I wanted to put the camera down and be there. I did; I was. Not just as an eye, but a heart and a mind and a cunt: a woman. I fancied the bride. Fair enough, that happens. Shrug, feel a little macho as I snap her picture, remind myself that smile isn't for me, it's for the album and the grandchildren. Claim it anyway, secretly. I fall a little bit in love with all of them, at their big moment.

So far, so good. Nothing to erase your feline smile, Cheshire one. This bride gave off a whiff of something blue, all right, and not in the traditional shade. Not to my nostrils anyway. Not that that's a first, either. But this was fresh and recent, unresigned. There was a moment just before she said her soft 'I do' when she seemed lost in a kind of mist under her veil. The pause became embarrassing, attacked but not quite punctured with coughs and throat-clearings.

The best photos are the ones you don't take. I began to assemble myself for a shot of what promised to be an event, but by the time I got there it was over, whatever it was. I wanted the expression I could just read, or so I thought, through the grating of her veil. She was somewhere else. Wool-gathering, as they say; gathering courage, I thought, to fracture the uneasy silence with a firm 'no', a *non serviam* that would surpass Lucifer's.

It was my damnable pride that ended the dream. I snapped the picture and the next moment I heard her low assent. I won't know what that expression was until I develop the picture; maybe not even then.

I trailed after the bridal procession despondently. It was all over. I was all wrong. I went to stand by the entrance to the marquee to snap them as they came towards me, smiling those ritual smiles. A child stood next to me. Then a real child screamed, and I looked again. The person next to me was leaning on sticks. Two halves of a broomstick, I identified. The face was hidden behind the mask of an ancient woman, skin craggy and lined, only the eyes her own. I knew she was a woman, though the whisper had gone up, by then, that the strange dwarfed thing was a friend of the groom's, playing a prank.

She wore a trenchcoat, an old gabardine one, backwards. Then the whisper changed. I heard the rumours around me like waves in the background. She was a woman scorned come to play spectre at the feast, a cast-off girlfriend of the groom's.

It was eminently possible. But what did Aristotle say? A probable impossibility is a better bet for drama than an improbable possibility. It was the probable impossibility I was interested in. It connected with that pregnant pause in the ceremony, with the look I thought I had seen on the bride's face.

It's you, I told myself sternly. Your tool is a camera, not a projector, so stop projecting. Don't get caught up in it. Take the pictures.

I was caught up, but I did take the pictures. She was always there in the corner of my eye. I saw her search the room as if for an ally. I felt her choose me, drawing me into the action. Shattering my neutrality. What neutrality?

We sat down and she proved to be probable and impossible, just as I'd thought. A glimpse behind the mask showed a young, tense face. The love story she told me was old as the hills, old as Demeter and Persephone, old as the news that kinder, kirche and kitchen always win out in the end. She was losing her anger, dissolving it in the champagne, dissipating her energy. I didn't want her to accept defeat. I didn't want her magnificent stand to be mere sniping, her courage to be just revenge. I thought she should go one step further and give it one last shot. Her best shot. Gather her grace and her guts and go over to Hermione, or whatever the hell the bride's name was. By now I felt quite hostile to *her*.

Frances. That's her name. The other one's Jane. She drank a little more and then she stood up on her sticks and pogo'd across the dance floor. I wished her well with all my heart, and made myself watch. I quailed for her. I couldn't just watch, but I didn't hide my head either, though I felt suddenly alone in a theatre with the terrible climax about to come. I picked up my camera. I got it all.

She trod lightly across the floor, clearing a path through the couples who rolled back for her obediently like the Red Sea for Moses. She smiled when she got close to Frances, I could see the smile under her mask and I hoped it showed in her eyes. Then she held out her hand to escort her to the dance floor, and Frances took it.

I got it; the smile, perceptible or not, the hand, the long walk to the dance floor while the band played on, oblivious. Probably thinking the bride was dancing with her grandmother. Her own mother looked livid, a red and blue dragon.

They danced the next three dances, talking all the time.

Even the band began scratching their heads. They kept playing fast feverish music as if to forestall a scandal. Then the bride and crone danced over to the bandstand to make a request. It was a long, slow, smoochy number. After it, they left.

I wanted to follow them, I wanted to run upstairs where I could hear them, in my mind's ear, giggling and kissing as they changed, both discarding their disguises. They didn't take long. I was tempted to go and say a word to the groom, who sat stroking his chin solemnly, blinking like a drunken owl. I felt a welling-up of compassion for him, but that was projection, I informed myself; because he was left out, too.

'Evelyn,' a laughing whisper came from the entrance and I followed it. Maybe it was wishful thinking; had they called me? Someone had summoned me. A picture had summoned me. It was the last picture, of the two of them leaning over the banisters with the bridal bouquet. Two kids in jeans, that's all they were, setting out together. I didn't have to wish them anything. They had it all.

I snapped, and Frances leaned over the banisters with clear intent. Then the huge great thing trailing ribbons like a jellyfish landed with a soft plop on the carpet. There wasn't time to put the camera down so I could catch it.

Jane handed it to me with a wink as they went out the door. I heard the motor, dully, bereft. It seemed more like a funeral suddenly. Who was I but a caretaker of memories, what was I undertaking with my arms clamped around a camera, instead of reaching for the magic bouquet?

An undertaker, not a caretaker. But I heard them roar away with a smile, thinking of the precious photographs I had. Thinking of the precious afternoon I'd just witnessed. That's what I was, when you came right down to it. A witness.

'We'll be in touch,' Frances had said. They would. Will they be a couple then, each singularly unavailable? Remains to be seen. I doubt that's their way.

I've been asleep, hunched here over the sink, my arm on a pile of equipment including the camera. I lift my arm; it's striped from the stuff I was lying on. So's my cheek. I can feel the grooves as I touch it. Funny how I love recording change. That's what I'm after. Yet I can't change my own stripes, even if I want to, sometimes. Solitary confinement in here, middle-aged dyke in love with a darkroom. Think I'll go get some fresh coffee before I start.

Notes on Weddings and Witches

I sat in the bright civility of a sunny St James's Park, waiting for Connie to come and eat a picnic lunch with me. The park was full of lovers, entwined or wishing they were, meeting for lunch from their offices and shops, valiantly pretending it was summer instead of a promising spring, while the fancy ducks on the lake looked peevish. The night before Connie and I had became lovers. No, too strong; the night before we had made love for the first time. Even that may be romanticizing; we still hadn't got these words right yet. It had been surprising; and whether we would do so again, and if so how often and with what intensity, was not yet established. I had known her for some time, liked her, an easy friendship somewhere between the truly intimate and the purely social. Last night we had had dinner together with a different friend. I had offered her a lift home.

My mind digressed here, fluttered perhaps by the warm breeze. Oh, the guilt of car owners: 'No, of course it's not out of my way, not really. I always go to Wandsworth via Stoke Newington.' It is still so hard for us middle-aged, middle-class lefties, left over from the bright sixties and the promise of Paris. We know with a well concealed bitterness that if by some amazing chance our youthful hopes are ever fulfilled we will not fully enjoy it having now entered into too much of the old kingdom and exchanged our squats for mortgages. I spent about a third of my life envying my less principled – or puritanical – contemporaries their success and another third deploring my own. The third third I spent not thinking about it at all because it is too sad saying farewell to all the brave promises, and driving people round London at all hours to expiate my guilt at being able to afford a car – albeit a seven-year-old Renault 6, carefully chosen to lack all possibility of chic, radical or otherwise.

So. I had offered her a lift home. In the car we got involved in some interesting, if bitchy, chat about the friend who'd given us dinner and allied subjects; so when we got to her flat she said to come in and have some coffee and I said yes please, and at that point I don't think honestly it had occurred to either of us, but before long it did, quite simply and imperatively. So I rang my husband and said I had got too drunk to drive home – which was, strictly speaking, probably true – so would it be all right if he got the kids off to school in the morning? Adultery has become radically simpler since our two daughters have been in school and can dress themselves and shove off nearly unaided and before my husband has to leave for work. Not that this is meant to imply that I go in for it a lot; in fact, before this particular night with Connie I had not slept with anyone at all for over eighteen months, which may of course have had something to do with it. Anyway he said oh fine, being a fine and trusting man, so there we were and it was fun and happy. I'm not sure if it will be relevant to the story, but yes, contrary to the best feminist principles I do actually deceive him – we have an adulterous rather than an 'open' marriage – and the only thing I can say in defence is that I don't think he really wants to know.

It was really very nice; and so was waking in the morning when the duties of hospitality were not mine, and no one was

32

going to ask where were their clean socks and/or last Thursday's homework and/or if I would please just this once feed the guinea-pig. And over coffee we both realized that she would have to rush off to work and I would have to rush back to my desk and it was all a little too abrupt and short-cut, and that it was a beautiful day, so we arranged to meet in St James's Park and have a picnic lunch together, which I would purchase – my turn for hospitality but at least I knew from dinner that she was not a vegetarian.

So there I was sitting in the park, my toes curling happily inside my boots knowing that soon it would be summertime and they would be able to come out and play. I did feel good. I felt lovely and happy, and before the feeling could diminish there she was walking across the funny little bridge towards me. It was a bit of a shock; the night before I had suddenly and completely desired her with a bright blue flame of harsh recognition and delight and watching her coming I couldn't imagine why – she was just this good and delightful woman I had known for some years. But when she got close I remembered, because she had a beautiful smile and lovely strong legs and a healthy tended-to body in which she walked with glee; and I felt that funny tight buzz in my tummy which is always my feeling of desire recalled and renewed. So we hugged, both trying to work out if we were lovers, or just better friends than we had been before, or if in fact as far as the other one had been concerned it had been a ghastly drunken error more embarrassing than anything else. I think the hug eliminated the last of these but did not clarify the others.

We sat on a bench – it really wasn't warm enough to sit on the grass – and ate the sloppy rolls I had prepared and opened the wine and gossiped. She told me, quite suddenly – although I suppose the subject of marriage was going to sneak in somewhere – a story she had heard about a woman who had gone to her ex-lover's – her ex-gay lover's –

wedding dressed as a witch. She had come all the way from Ireland, uninvited and dressed up as an aged and ugly crone in order to blight the wedding. At first I was impressed. It seemed a fine and dramatic gesture; certainly I could well imagine how efficiently it would have blighted my wedding if any of my women ex-lovers had pulled such a stunt. And this, according to Connie, had been at a rather smart wedding with marquee and all in the dappled summer garden in the country. Served the bride right, said Connie decisively, but throwing me a careful glance despite her emphasis.

Actually there are always witches at weddings, no one needs to dress up as one, I told Connie and remembered with a blush of pure horror about Clare's wedding. Clare had 'come out' at about the same time as I did when we were students together, but had snuck back in again rather sooner. She had been bolder, and her young man a nice well trained new-left good-guy, and she had invited us all to the wedding. And we had gone, some of us, to this little wedding, also in the country, but discreetly. Perhaps they hadn't wanted to let their daughter's friends upset their charming social acquaintances because there had been about six of us, Clare's people, and a few of his – the groom's – friends and quite discrepantly, socially speaking, a handful of relatives and close friends of her parents. It was uneasy to start with, I told Connie, as you can imagine, and Mira had got drunk. As the wedding breakfast got underway Mira had got drunker and drunker. At first it had been okay, a bit much, you know, but containable; she had been full of what They, the grown-ups, might just about have taken for wizard pranks, which if not ladylike at least had tradition on their side. Although the things she smeared on the car with lipstick bordered on the obscene, they weren't noticeably worse than what Clare's brothers were writing. It was that sort of wedding. But after the happy couple had departed to honeymoon bliss, she went completely over the edge. Coleridge's Ancient Mariner had not a patch on her, though I've never been able to read it since without feeling passionately for the wedding guests. If she had just stopped one in three it might still have been possible, but she stood in the drawing-room and declaimed. She said that the only reason that Clare was getting married instead of living out her life as a happy dyke was because she had been consistently, continually, sexually assaulted by her father, and that her mother had done nothing, nothing whatever, to protect her daughter from what she must have known was happening. That Clare was therefore incapable of trusting women and had come to believe that men had power and that she would need a man to protect her from the power of her own guilt. The awful thing, the truly awful thing, had been . . . no, wait, there were two quite separate truly awful things. The first was that it was quite obviously, absolutely blindingly clear that this was true. The Bastard stood there in his morning coat and you could see that it was true. And Mira, who is tiny and had obviously meant to behave herself because she was wearing a reasonable approximation to respectable wedding clothes, shouted at him and at all of us for what seemed like half an hour the intimate details of his incestuous liaison with his daughter and he could not say one damned thing because it was so patently true. But that was not the worst: the worst was that her spell enchanted *us* too, so that instead of being furious and angry with the smug bourgeois child-molester as we ought to have been, or with Clare's mother, of whom it was equally true as Mira went on to inform the assembled guests – that she had done nothing about these goings-on because of the social embarrassment it would have entailed; oh no, we were exposed in all our complicity – we tried to shut her up. Seized by embarrass-ment as great as everyone else's, we did not join her, support her, or in any way endorse her. We tried to make her stop; and finally Sophie and I took her away in disgrace like a little girl who has got over-excited at a birthday party. Yes, and bloody apologized to the parents, making little tsk-tsk noises about our friend not having a good head for alcohol. We preferred their lie over Mira's truth because although we thought we were fancy revolutionaries, the business of behaving at weddings was too strong, too deep, too embedded. And still, as I told Connie this story, fairly unembellished and accurately, I was not sure whether my embarrassment was for failing Mira, for failing Clare, for failing the principles by which we claimed to live; or whether it was still that deep social shame that someone should be so vulgar as to draw attention to themselves, and by association *me*, at a nice country wedding. So you see, I said, there isn't any need to dress up as a witch, she'll be there. Mira put an evil spell on all of us; even on Clare, because the marriage didn't live happily ever after, and how could it after such a bewitchment?

There was a pause. A long pause. Connie was looking at the ducks. Then she said, Why did you marry him anyway? And she had the right to ask because after all it was less than twenty-four hours since she had run not the top but the side of her thumb across my stretch-marks with fascination and amazement and observed with tenderness and accuracy that the base of my stomach looked like a crumpled piece of crêpe paper that someone had sprinkled water on. And I, as well as she, deserved a proper answer; that I have learned in ten years of marriage.

To kill the witch, of course.

In all the best stories it tells you. The witch is killed, the witch dies at the wedding. There is no other escape; you can go and live in the hills for years with the dwarfs, who can love you and look after you and take care of you and give you useful domestic responsibilities but it won't do you any good; the witch will still be alive and well and plotting against you. But the prince can just turn up, all of a sudden without merit or causality and, so long as he lays on a wedding, that does for the witch. The very end of *Little Snow White* says it clearly: 'Then the wicked woman uttered a curse, and was so wretched, so utterly wretched that she knew not what to do. At first she would not go to the wedding at all, but she had no peace, and had to go and see the young Queen. And when she went in, she recognized Snow White; and she stood still with rage and fear and could not stir. But iron slippers had already been put upon the fire, and they were brought in with tongs, and set before her. Then she was forced to put on the red-hot shoes and dance until she dropped down dead.'

You know it by heart? said Connie.

Oh yes, I know it by heart; that's Grimm, but there are lots of others.

Well, she said, go on.

Go on? I said. Just going that far had left me curiously weary though I was glad the witch metaphor had been available, as it were already prepared on the fire.

Yes, she said, what witch? Who is the witch? Your mother?

I wanted to digress again, to tell her most wittily that she was a Freudian Reductionist or something, and perhaps the red-hot slippers were symbols of something altogether more fun. But it was sunny in the park and a good sweet day; and I knew too closely how wicked and witch-like straight women who play at gay sex are, and how I did not have the right, at least for this one lunchtime, to play those games, even though quite possibly Connie would not have minded and would have played along too. I do not like honesty, frankness, openness; it is a social mode that I deplore really, I prefer playing games and spinning juggling balls in the air, magical illusion. That is probably why I write fiction as a matter of fact. No, I do not like the confessional style, though I will now add that Connie had a beautiful, slightly raised mole, very dark brown, in her arm-pit, not on the body side of the hair but on that very soft delicate skin on the lower inside of the arm, like a tiny drop of melted non-milk chocolate accidentally dropped there for the purpose of being licked off.

But, given the circumstances she deserved honesty, as I have explained above, and I had the witch image all set up, so I decided to give it a go. No, no I said, not my mother. How woefully ingnorant of you; the witch is never the mother, always the step-mother, the mother at one remove. Though of course the step-mother has to get rid of the real mother first, or work through her, doesn't she?

Connie looked irritated; she did not quite say oh get on with it, but she very nearly did. I don't think she liked being called woefully ignorant, for which I could not blame her.

Do you really not know about the witch? The witch is the strong bad woman inside me; inside, I thought, everyone. She is bad and mad, and if you don't get rid of her she will eat you up. She thought she had eaten Snow White up when the huntsman brought in the deer's heart and lungs for her, and she was very happy. She didn't want Snow White to grow up and be a beautiful happy woman. The witch is very beautiful and self-sufficient. She looks into her mirror and says 'Looking glass, looking glass on the wall/ Who in this land is the fairest of all?' and the answer she wants is You are, you, you, you. And of course that won't do at all because if we all, all we strong women, came to believe we were the fairest of all what would happen to all the children who need mummies and all the grown up men who need mummies and all the nice women who need a touch of mummying so that they can be mummies themselves? So they hunt the witch, and they make her wear red-hot slippers and dance until she drops dead. When I touched on my own witch power I was scared, I was scared both ways. I could smell the cooking flesh right the way through from the middle-ages, the flesh of the burning feet in the red-hot slippers that have to be handled with tongs, the flesh of the women burned at the stake, it sizzles and roasts and goes on roasting for eternity. Civilized people kill witches to make the world safe for civilization and I was afraid of that. But that was not the real fear, though it is a real fear, I mean it was not the most central fear, what they might do to me if I claimed my power. The real fear was of the witch herself, the witch in me. I knew, you see, I knew that I could name the name of God which is unnamable and so escape from Eden, like Lilith did who is the great witch of the Bible literature, but that if I did I would have to go out into the hot tearing desert, I would have to live there in my own power and glory. I would be the woman clothed with the sun, with the moon at her feet and crowned with the stars. I would know the spells of summoning and the spells of exorcizing and I would have to use them. The witch would eat me up and take me in and there would be no space, no space for littleness and pettiness. There was the risk she would devour me, and I would be left crazy, crazy. I touched base with that briefly in a mental hospital once and I knew that I did not want so much power. Like Clare, like Clare, I wanted someone who was powerful enough to control the power in me. I was simply and straightforwardly scared of the power that I might have. I really do not want to be one of the three prophets who walk in the furnace through the night, and the Holy One is with them and they don't get burned. I really wanted to be the sort of ordinary person who went to the supermarket with a shopping trolley and would frazzle and frizzle into cigarette-ash at the mere sight of a firey furnace. This does sound a bit mad, doesn't it? I suppose I just found the power of being free too much for me. I was scared out of my mind, literally, giddy and reeling with possibility, and that didn't seem very practical. I wanted to be re-anchored, weighted down with reality, with normality. So, you see, I read it up in all the spell books and they all told me that a wedding with a true prince, carefully selected, would deal with the witch once and for all, so I got married. I think perhaps I should sue them under the Trades Descriptions Act. But I was quite young and quite frail, and I thought, I mean I hoped, that marriage would deal with it all for ever, I mean all the harsh and perilous witch stuff. So I sold my witchy inheritance for a mess of pottage and thought I could live, calm and sane and untouched by it all, happily ever after. Do you understand at all?

And, rather to my surprise, Connie said that Yes she did understand. When I was the age, she said, that you were when you got married I knew perfectly well that I was gay, I never questioned that as a matter of fact, not at all; but I did not like it, I did not like it at all, it did not make me happy. I thought, I wanted, I desperately wanted to be fifty. I thought that being fifty would be the spell. I thought that when I was fifty it would all go away and be over, done with, just go away and not be a hurt and a bother any more. She grinned. I'm forty-six now and it doesn't show any signs of doing so. I don't think my spell is going to work. Did yours?

Now *I* grinned. No. No, it didn't. As you may have noticed. First it just put me under another enchantment: the spell of being a Good Woman. I worked, I worked like hell on making that work, you know. Of course more detailed reading led me to suppose that sometimes the witch is only really dealt with when the son-and-heir was born, so I tried that. Actually I had the girls instead, and they themselves are wonderful, but it didn't work in the sense that you mean. Of course not. Because of course all the stories are a con – to lure us to the wedding. And the real purpose of the wedding is to turn us, hey-presto and abracadabra, not even into real princesses but into Walt-Disney-Snow-White-Clones, infantilized, sweet and hopeless. And even that never quite took. I go on wavering, not making it as a good woman, wanting the more tasteful bits of my own power, wanting a taste of the apples of Eden, wanting the knowledge of good and evil, as opposed to real goodness, purity of commitment, either way, either way.

Yes, said Connie. Ay, there's the rub. If it were done when 'tis done, then 'twere well it were done quickly. (You can see from this nimbleness at least one of the reasons why I really did like her a lot, because it is not easy to throw in a thing like that, and appositely to boot.) That's the rub, she continued. Because anyone who knows the stories knows damn well that you can't nibble. Six seeds are enough to keep you in thrall to the great power of the dark.

She smiled, not unkindly. We looked at each other for a moment, with some horror at the improper places this conversation had led us to. Part of me wanted to start weeping, to lie on her shoulder, invite her arms, be a poor little victim of male chauvinism and psychic disorder. To make her want to make me a Cause. I had to stiffen every sinew of self-respect and also of affection for her, not to do that. Not to do it again and stir up, again, merry hell in my own life and in the lives I can too easily suck at. It was a bit of a struggle.

I am not a converter, said Connie. I never have been, not sexually. I'm not even going to ask why you stay with him now. I don't want you to tell me.

Okay, I said, I won't.

We got up together. I gathered up the paper bags from the picnic and as we walked along the path I threw them into a litter bin. We had not given one crumb to a single passing sparrow, let alone encouraged any to come and sit on our heads. Given the circumstances I think that reflects considerable credit on both of us. After we had walked a little way Connie said, How do you feel about one-night stands?

An extremely inexact description, I replied, but if they're like last night's then they're very good. I knew what she was saying and immediately I was overwhelmed with desire for her, with a greed to see that dark mole again and to wake in her sunny flat with her oddly soft arms around me. But I was brought up to have impeccable manners.

She said, I don't want it, I just don't want it, your witch or your spells. There's something I didn't tell you, you see. That story I began with, about the woman who dressed up for her friend's wedding: they left together, they ran away from the reception and are still living together. The witch and the bride.

I was livid. Truly furious. Apart from all the other things, if you're the author you really don't expect other people to pull a twist at the end of your own short story. And also, well, it was a judgment on me. However richly deserved.

But she was, not unreasonably, rather pleased with herself. And I could not blame her. She did not crow, though, she was generous. Look, she said, I'm forty-six years old and I have a life which I like a lot, and I'm not willing to go travelling in your crazy places with you. I think if you really want to kill the witch you had better find a younger woman, a woman with more energy and less investment.

The last woman I went to bed with, I said sadly, was exactly the same amount younger than me that you are older; she said the same thing, in the end, only exactly in reverse. And my good manners prevented me from adding that that was at least one of the reasons why I stayed with him, because that was something she did not want to know.

We stomped along for about another thirty yards, and then suddenly, most surprisingly, a bubble of delight surged up in me, because it had been good the night before and because the sunshine was promising the summer, and because there were women who had beautiful moles in their arm-pits and could still tease you, listen to you, hope for you; and because after all I just felt wonderful. Connie, I said, oh Connie, I do like you.

Thank God for that, she said and gave me a nice hug. Look, I have to get back to the office. Will I see you at Mira's party?

Shit, I said, do you know her? But I couldn't help laughing, with considerable admiration. It really was even better than the ending to her wedding story.

Oh yes. She grinned wickedly, teasing me now, being older and wiser and triumphant, and also warmed by sunniness and the delicate perfume of my delight-bubble. Oh yes, very well. And I've heard her version of the Clare wedding story.

My imagination was seized. I thought, even as we stood there in St James's Park, that I could write all three stories, Mira's, Clare's and the observing friend's. Or I could go home and wrestle out this story, about what it means to be married and sleep with other women and be a feminist and feel guilty about owning a car and to be scared of my own witch power. Perhaps it would work better if I tackled it some completely different way. Perhaps I could just tell a story about a witch at a wedding, simply, stolidly, like the old women who narrated for Grimm Bros Ltd. Perhaps, I should stuff this contemporary relevance and convincing social detail and just rewrite the story of Persephone in Hell, the witch at her own wedding, and hype it up with the florid and giddy language which is permitted when you touch on mythological themes. I'm not sure. I know I have to keep trying. With the witch and with the stories.

THE SIN STORIES

A Fall from Grace

Those years the children – in Brittany, Bordeaux and the Loire valley, even as far away as the Low Countries, Andalusia and the Riviera – missed their acrobats. In the Circus the dingy wild animals, the clowns, illusionists and freaks remained, but earthbound. Gravity held the Circus, and the mud, the stench and the poverty were more evident. The magic-makers, the sequinned stars that flashed and poised and flew and sparkled through the smoke above the watchers' heads, the death-defiers who snatched the Circus from the mud and turned it into flowers and frissons, were gone.

Gone away to the strange camp on the Champs de Mars, where they were needed to help Monsieur E. build his beautiful tower. Oh, the local residents might tremble in their beds with fear at the fall from heaven; intellectuals and artists might protest that 'Paris is defaced by this erection'. But the Circus people, the artists of body and philosophers of balance (with wild libidinous laughs at so unfortunate and accurate a turn of phrase), they understood; the acrobats – without words and with a regular fifty centimes an hour – knew. They alone could comprehend the vision. They knew in the marrow of their bones and the tissue of their muscles the precise tension – that seven million threaded rods, and two and half million bolts could, of course, hold fifteen thousand steel girders in perfect balance. With sinews and nerves and cartilage they did it nightly: that tension and harmony against gravity was their stock-in-trade. Their great delight was that Monsieur E., a gentleman, a scientist, knew it too, and knew that they knew and needed them to translate his vision. High above Paris they swooped and caracoled, rejoicing in the delicacy and power of that thrust, upwards, away from the pull of the ground. And so they left their Circuses, sucked towards Paris by a dream that grew real under their authority – and for two years the acrobats and trapeze artists and highwire dancers and trampolinists abandoned their musical illusions to participate in historical, scientific reality.

Eva and Louise too came to Paris. Not that they were allowed to mount up ever higher on the winches, hanging beside the cauldrons which heated the bolts white hot; not that they were permitted to balance on the great girders, shifting their weight so accurately to swing the heavy strands of lace into place. Their skill, as it happens, was not in doubt, but they were women. They drifted northwards, almost unthinkingly, with their comrades and colleagues, simply because the power of Monsieur E.'s vision was magnetic and all the acrobats were drawn inwards by it and Eva and Louise were acrobats. And they lived with the other acrobats on the Champs de Mars, poised between aspiration and reality, and the city of Paris went to their heads and they were, after a few months, no longer who they had been when they came.

Their Circus had been a disciplined nursery for such children. Born to it, they had known its rhythms, its seductions and its truths from the beginning. Precious to their parents because identical twins are good showbusiness, they were only precious inasmuch as they worked and made a show. With each lurching move of the travelling caravans they had had to re-create the magic from the mud. Only after the hours of sweat and struggle with the tent, with the law, with the unplanned irregularities of topography, and with costumes which had become muddy or damp or creased or torn – only then were they able to ascend the snaking ladders and present the New Creation, where fear and relief were held in perfect tension; where the immutable laws of nature – gravity and pendula arches, weight, matter and velocity – were apparently defied but in fact bound, utilized, respected and controlled; where hours of dreary practice, and learning the capacities and limits of self and other, where the disciplines of technique and melodrama and precision were liberated suddenly and briefly into glamour and panache. And still were only a complete part of a delicately balanced and complete whole which included the marionette man, the clowns, the seedy lions and the audience itself.

But Paris, and a Paris in which they could not do what they were trained to do, was a holiday, a field day, where the rewards were quick and detached from the labour. As the tower grew so did Eva and Louise, but the tower was anchored and they were free floating. They learned to cross the laughing river and seek out the *boîtes* of Montmartre. Here, their white knickers and petticoats frothed easily in the hot water now available to them, they learned to dance the new dance – the cancan. Here their muscularity, their training, their athleticism stood them in good stead. They were a hit; with the management who paid them to come and show off round bosoms, shapely legs, pink cheeks and bleached petticoats; with the clientele whose oohs and ahhs were more directly appreciative than those of any Circus audience.

Yes, the beauty and the energy of them as they danced and pranced and watched the tower grow and watched their comrades labour upwards. They walked under the spreading legs of the tower and laughed at the jokes called down to them; they ran among the tents and teased the labourers; they turned the odd trick here and there for affection and amusement, although they could get better paid across the river where the rich men lived. Monsieur E., coming each day to see how his dream was developing, soon learned their names and would stop and smile for them, and they smiled back, arms entwined with each other, but eyes open for everything that was going on in the world. And they reassured him of his beauty, his virility, his potency, all of which he was manifesting in his tower which broke the rules of nature by the authority of science and the power of men. One day he told them, for the simple pleasure of saying it, for he knew they were simple girls and simply would not understand, that when his tower was finished it would weigh less than the column of air that contained it. The girls laughed and wanted to know why then it would not fly away, and he laughed too, indulgently, and explained, paternally, about displacement. But from then on the idea of the tower simply, ooh-la-la, flying away with them was fixed in Eva and Louise's minds and it made them laugh because of course they knew that it was impossible.

And walking in the streets and parks they learned new styles of dressing and new styles of living; and their eyes were wide and bright with delight. Having little to do all day they wandered here and there, through boulevards and over bridges. In the flower markets they were overcome by the banks of sweetness, the brilliance of colours; in the antique-shop windows they saw the bright treasures from China and Egypt, from far away and long ago; and in the cafés they smelled new smells and heard raffish conversations about things they had not even dreamed of. And everywhere they went, because they looked so alike and smiled so merrily and were always together, people came to recognize them and smile at them, and they felt loved and powerful and free as they had never felt before. All Paris was their friend and the city itself was their Paradise.

They were a hit too in the *Salons des Femmes*, where the strange rich women, who dressed like men and caressed Eva and Louise like men too, were delighted by their health and energy and innocence. And by their professional willingness to show off. Louise enjoyed these evenings when they drank tiny glasses of jewel-coloured drinks and performed – dances, tumbles, stage acrobatics – and were petted and sent home in carriages. But Eva felt nervous and alarmed; and also drawn, excited, elated and it was not just the coloured concoctions that made her giggle all the way back to the Champs de Mars and swear that they would not go again. In the dark warmth of the bed they shared, Eva's arms would wind round Louise as they had done every night since they were conceived, but her fingers crackled with new electricity and she wondered and wanted and did not want to know what she wanted.

And of course they did go again, because it was Paris and the Spanish chestnut flowers stood out white on the trees like candles and the air was full of the scent of them, giddy, dusty, lazy. At night the city was sparkling and golden and high above it the stars prickled, silver and witty. And Monsieur E.'s tower, taut and poised was being raised up to join the two together. In the hot perfumed houses they were treated as servants, as artists and as puppy dogs, all together, and it confused them, turned their heads and enchanted them. One evening, watching them, the Contessa della Colubria said to her hostess, 'Well Celeste, I think they won't last long, those two. They'll become tawdry and quite spoiled. But they are very charming.' 'I don't know,' Celeste said, 'they are protected. By their work of course, but not that; it must be primal innocence to love, to be one with another person from the beginning, with no desires, no consciousness.' 'Innocence? Do you think so? Perhaps it is the primal sin, to want to stay a child, to want to stay inside the first embrace, the first cell.' The Contessa's eyes glittered like her emeralds. 'Do you think it might be interesting to find out?' Celeste turned away from her slightly, watching Eva and Louise across the salon; she said quickly, 'Ah, *ma mie*, leave them be. They are altogether too young for you to bother with.' The Contessa laughed, 'But Celeste, you know how beguiled I am by innocence. It attracts me.'

She was mysterious, the Contessa della Colubria, strange and fascinating; not beautiful *mais très chic*, clever, witty, and fabulously wealthy. She had travelled, apparently everywhere, but now lived alone in Paris, leaving her husband in his harsh high castle in Tuscany and challenging the bourgeois gossips with her extravagance, her outré appearance and the musky sensation of decadence. Rumour followed her like a shadow, and like a shadow had no clear substance. It was known that she collected the new paintings, and Egyptian curios and Chinese statues; it is said that she also collected books which respectable people would not sully their homes with, that she paid fabulous sums to actresses for ritual performances, that she slid along the side of the pit of the unacceptable with a grace that was uncanny. But she had created a social space for herself in which the fear, the feeling, that she was not nice, not quite safe, became unimportant.

She took Eva and Louise home in her carriage that night. Sitting between them, her arms around each neck, her legs stretched out, her long narrow feet braced against the floor, her thin face bland, only her elongated ophidian eyes moving. The sharp jewel she wore on her right hand cut into Louise's neck, but she did not dare to say anything. The Contessa told them stories.

'You see the stars,' she said, and they were bright above the river as the carriage crossed over it. 'Long ago, long long ago it was thought that each star was a soul, the soul of a beautiful girl, too lovely to die, too bright to be put away in the dark for ever. The wild Gods of those times did not think that so much beauty should be wasted, you see. Look at that star up there, that is Cassiopeia, she was a queen and so lovely that she boasted she was more beautiful than the Nerides, the sea-nymphs, and they in their coral caves were so jealous and angry that they made Neptune their father punish her. But the other Gods were able to rescue her and throw her up to heaven and make her safe and bright.

'And those stars there, those are Ariadne's crown; it was given to her by Bacchus who was the God of wine and passion, not an orderly God, not a good God at all, but fierce and beautiful. Ariadne loved Theseus first, who was a handsome young man, and she rescued him from a terrible monster called the Minotaur who lived in a dark maze and ate people. Ariadne gave her lover a thread so he could find his way out and a sword so he could kill the monster. But he wasn't very grateful, as men so seldom are, and he left her on an island called Naxos.'

'I know those ones,' said Louise, pointing, breaking the soft flow of the Contessa's voice with an effort, 'those ones up there, those are the Seven Sisters who preferred to be together.'

'The Pleiades, yes, how clever you are. And you see that one of them is dimmer than the others. That is Meriope, and her star is faint because she married, she married a mortal, but the rest are bright and shiny.'

Louise's neck hurt from the Contessa's sharp ring. She felt tired and uneasy. She wanted to sit with Eva, their arms around each other, tight and safe. She did not understand the Contessa. But Eva liked the stories, liked the arm of the Contessa resting warm against her skin, admired the sparkling of emeralds and eyes and was lulled, comfortable and snug, in the smooth carriage.

The balance shifted. They knew about this. As Eva leaned outwards and away, away from the centre, then Louise had to move lower, heavier, tighter, to keep the balance. As

Louise pulled inward, downward, Eva had to stretch up and away to keep the balance. On the tightrope they knew this; but it was a new thing for them. There was another way, of course; their parents had had an act based on imbalance, based on difference, based on his heavy grounding and her light flying, the meeting-place of the weighty and the floating. But they had not learned it. Even in the gravity-free place where they had first learned to dance together, in the months before they were born, it had been turning in balance, in precise sameness. It was the poise of symmetry that they knew about; the tension of balance. And it was foolhardy always to change an act without a safety net and with no rehearsals. They did not know how to discuss it. The difference was painful, a tightening, a loss of relaxation, of safety. The acrobat who was afraid of falling would fall. They knew that. But also the acrobat who could not believe in the fall would fall. They knew that too.

The Contessa took them to a smart pâtisserie on the Champs-Elysées. She bought them frothing hot chocolate, and they drank it with glee, small moustaches of creamy foam forming on their pink upper lips. They were laughing and happy. 'Which of you is the older,' she asked, 'which was born first?' 'We don't know,' said Eva and giggled, 'No one knows. We tumbled out together and the woman who was supposed to be with my mother was drunk and she got muddled up and no one knows.' 'If they did it would not matter,' said Louise. 'Our mother says we were born to the trade, we dived out with elegance.' Eva and Louise were pleased with themselves today, with the distinction of their birth, with their own inseparability, with the sweetness of the chocolate and the lightness of the little apricot tartlettes. The smart folk walked by on the pavement outside, but they were inside and as pretty as any grand lady. And in the bright spring sunlight the Contessa was not strange and dangerous, she was beautiful and glamorous, she was like something from a fairy story who had come into their lives and would grant them wishes and tell them stories.

The Contessa came in her new toy, her automobile, roaring and dangerous, to seek them out on the Champs de Mars. She was driven up in her bright new chariot, and stopped right between the legs of the tower. The acrobats swarming up and down, labouring, sweating and efficient, swung aside to make space for her, as she uncoiled herself from the seat and walked among them. And she knew Monsieur E. and gave him a kiss and congratulated him on his amazing edifice. Louise did not like to see her there, but she invited them into her car and they rode off to the admiring whistles of their friends. 'In Russia,' the Contessa told them, 'the people ride in sleighs across the snow and the wolves howl at them, but it does not matter because they are snugly wrapped in great furs and the horses pull them through the dark, because it is dark all winter in Russia, and the motion of the sleigh is smooth and the furs are warm and they fall asleep while the horses run and the night is full of vast silences and strange noises so that they hang bells on the horses' bridles, and all the nobility speak in French, so that people will know how civilized they are, and not mistake them for the bearded warriors who live in snow houses beyond the northern stars. And even the women of these people wear high leather boots and ride with the men on short-legged, fierce horses. They ride so well up in that strange land that ordinary people have come to believe that they and their horses are one: they call them Centaurs, horses with human heads and trunks and arms. Long, long ago there were real Centaurs who roamed in Anatolia and knew strange things and would sometimes take little babies and train them in their ways and they would grow up wise and strong and fit to be rulers, because the Centaurs taught them magic, but for ordinary people the Centaurs were very dangerous because they were neither people nor animals, but monsters.'

And they rode in the Contessa's car around the Bois and she took them back to her house and taught them how to sniff up a white powder through slender silver straws and then they could see green-striped tigers prowling across the Contessa's garden with eyes like stars, and butterflies ten feet across with huge velvet legs that fluttered down from the trees like falling flowers. And when they went home they found they could believe that Monsieur E.'s tower could fly, and they could fly on it, away away to a warm southern place, but they did not want to leave Paris, so they waved to the tower and they were laughed at for being drunk, and they did not tell anyone about the white powder.

One day at a party, in a new beautiful strange house where they had been invited to do a little show, the Contessa sought out Eva for one brief moment when she was alone and said, 'I have a pretty present for you.' 'Yes, Madame.' 'See it is earrings.' She held out her long, thin, dry hand, the palm flat and open, and there was a pair of earrings, two perfect little gold apples. 'These are golden apples from the garden of the Hesperides; Juno, the queen of all the Gods, gave them to Jupiter, the king of all the Gods, for a wedding present. They grow in a magical garden beyond the edge of the world and they are guarded by the four beautiful daughters of Atlas who carries the world on his back. And around the tree they grow on lies a huge horrible dragon who never sleeps. So you see they are very precious.' Eva looked at them, amused; she had little interest in their value, but liked their prettiness. 'One for me and one for Louise, Madame?' she asked. 'No, both are for you. But you will have to come by yourself one evening to my house and collect them.' 'But Madame, we always go together, you know that.' 'Eva,' smiled the Contessa, 'I'll tell you a little story: once there was a woman and she was expecting a baby, and she wished and wished good things for her baby and especially that it would grow up to have good manners. Well her pregnancy went on and on, and on and on, and still the baby was not born. And none of the wise doctors could make any sense of it. And in the end, ever more pregnant, after many many years, as a very ancient lady she died of old age. So the doctors who were of course very curious opened her up and they found two little ladies, quite more than middle-aged, sitting beside the birth door saying with perfect good manners, "After you," and "No, no, my dear, after *you*". *C'est très gentille*, but what a waste, what a waste, don't you think?' Eva giggled at the silly story, covering her mouth with her hand like a child. She did not care about the earrings but she knew that if she went to the Contessa she would find out, she would find out what it was she did not know, what it was that made her nervous and elated. She could feel too the weight of Louise, the weight of Louise inward on both of them, the weight swinging out of balance. She had to correct that inward weight with an outward one. Had to remake the balance, the inward weight with an outward one. Also she wanted to know, and if she went she would know that and something else perhaps.

'Yes, Madame,' she said, 'yes, I will come.'

And the Contessa smiled.

She did not know how to tell Louise. She could not find any words for what and why; they have never needed words before, they have not rehearsed any. Next Tuesday she would go to visit the Contessa. This week she had to find words to tell Louise. Instead she drank. Louise, who knew she was excited but could not feel why, could not understand, could not pull Eva back to her, drank too. Their comrades on the Champs de Mars thought it was funny to see the girls drunk; they plied them with brandy and wine. Drunk, Eva and Louise showed off, they performed new tricks, leaping higher, tumbling, prancing; they do not stumble or trip, they cannot stumble or trip. They are beautiful and skilful. This is their place. The men clap for them, urging them on. In the space under the tower they dance and frolic. They start to climb, swinging upwards; from each other's hands they ascend. Somersaulting, delighting, they follow the upward thrust of the tower; its tension, its balance is theirs. The voices of the men fade below. Once, as they rise above seven hundred feet, they falter. 'It's your fault,' says Eva, 'you lean in too hard.' 'No, says Louise, 'it is you, you are too far out.' But they find their rhythm again, trusting the rhythm of the tower that Monsieur E. and their hard-worked colleagues below have structured for them. On the other side of the river they can see Paris, spread out for them now, the islands in the Seine floating on the dark water, the gay streets shining with golden lights. Above, the sky is clear: the moon a bright dying fingernail, the constellations whizzing in their glory. The tower seems to sway, sensitive to their need. It is not quite finished, but as they approach the top they are higher than they have ever been, they are climbing and swinging and swooping upwards. Suddenly both together they call out to one another, 'It was my fault, I'm sorry.' The rhythm is flowing now, their wrists linked, trusting, knowing, perfect. It is their best performance ever. Down below the men still watch, although it is too dark to see. They know they will never see another show like this. They know these two are stars. They make no error. They do not fall. They fly free, suddenly, holding hands, falling stars, a moment of unity and glory.

But it is three hundred yards to ground and afterwards no one is able to sort out which was which or how they could be separated.

Green Tea

'Where is the Herbalist?'

She rows towards me through the fog, her long arms dipping as she peers, looking for the source of all the noise. It's the thunderous lorries on the Lee Road; that should be apparent to anyone. Also apparent to me is that another noise comes from her, a tinkling of bells from the miniature belfry of her throat, a private Evensong choired and rung by string after string of beads and bells that pull energetically on their ropes as she walks. She's draped with emblems of the 'sixties like a flower warrior just come out of hiding in the hills, unaware that the war of the daffodils has long been over. Her place, if she has one, is alongside the others on windy street-corners handing out dry paper flowers on certain days marked out for remembrance.

'The *Herbalist*,' she insists, then smiles. 'Do you know where the Herbalist's shop is?' Her skirt swishes round her ankles under a long royal-blue cape.

'No.' I don't even know *what* a herbalist's shop is. That is, I *know*, of course. Just the requisite amount to make an informed decision to know no more. I walk on; she melts away entirely, into the fog.

The fog hangs on for a few days, exempting me, I decide,

from my usual two-mile daily walk, meant to ward off the rolls of fat threatening to engulf my waist, also meant to fortify my nerves, which are increasingly shaky these last few years. I'm all right in my room, but the longer I remain there the less I want to leave. Survival depends on maintaining some degree of readiness to emerge. There's a shop on the corner stocked with everything, up and down the scale from soap to booze and back again – my usual progression. I can charge up there, but there's something sordid and ratlike about my raids, breathless, a coat pulled hastily over my clothes, my moth-eaten lived-in or perhaps unlived-in clothes. So I make myself take a brisk walk down the heavily laden Lee Road. If I can keep it up, I tell myself, gritting my teeth as the mammoths growl past, I'll have the problem licked.

What a marvellous performance it is, the disappearing trick of the fog. The outer world merely hinted at, almost erased. The inner world eased into its rightful prominence and place. Not only is there no longer any need to go anywhere, there is no longer anywhere *to* go.

The bells! Once more she moves in her trancelike way beneath my windows, a time traveller from forgotten hallucinatory days. Roving the fog; perhaps it's her medium as well, poor creature, perhaps she's one of the many casualties of that era condemned to wander aimlessly, to rove, aiming hopelessly at 'the Herbalist'. The strings of bells around her neck fall oddly silent, like lace made of cobwebs. Even her clogs are muffled on the pavement, as if the fog were a sort of sound-proofing.

And yet she distracts me. From what? From nothing, and nothing is my preferred portion. She takes me with her through the fog into another day, where I most emphatically do not want to go. Where I most emphatically cannot resist the chance to go.

Once I was an ordinary working bachelor, catching sight

of the ordinary women watching me on my late-night shopping expeditions, licking their lips, taking note of my puzzlement over the problem of a week's solitary menus. I paraded these things, the puzzlement and the solitude, as stylishly as I could. I picked up many a lay and even made a few friends on those evenings. I had friends, then; curious thought. Infinitely more curious than the other; I got laid, then.

It all changed, irreversibly, when I came across, not on a shopping trip, oh, no! the girl I'd saved myself for. The girl I'd been practising for. Why do I say 'girl'? For the romance of the word. She resented it, but I clung, only sometimes persuaded to the more formal romance of 'lady'. 'Woman' I could not pronounce. When I met her my dimly lit interior was floodlighted, starlighted. Then plunged into total darkness, when she left.

The bed is there, in the alcove. The bottle is beneath it. The bed is not there, really. That is to say, once it docked there, in the harbour of the alcove. Now it is sunk there, a collection of unpleasant parasites, rotting planks, cheesy sheets. I myself am a failing, flaking substance, and the bed reflects this. It's the only thing that does. There are no mirrors here. I shattered them all the day she left.

The absence of mirrors is, surprisingly, among my most severe penances. Whether I do penance for loving her or for losing her, I don't know. Sometimes I feel one is the greater sin, sometimes the other. I shall know at the Judgement. There had better be one! To remain ignorant of precisely where and when one went wrong, of the exact split second one's fate was sealed, to fail to locate the first tremor of hopelessness on the seismograph of the soul – the depths of such ignorance would be hellish indeed. The one hellish consolation is, of course, that should it be so, one will not need to think about it; indeed, one will not even be tempted to think about it.

The girl strolls back through the fog, which now mixes with dusk. What sweet musk they make together. Did I say *musk*? *Her* perfume, of course. I see resemblances everywhere. An indication of genius, to Aristotle, whom I must assume did not suffer from the affliction. A trail of hair, a catch in a voice; I look, I listen, I proceed, shaking my head. I have always been susceptible to metaphorical encounters, that is, I always was. The susceptibility passed, as all other susceptibilities passed, when she . . . till now. As the belled girl draws her scent of musk through the fog, I must cower and describe, thrown back on the horrible prepositions, those weak, weak joints trying to hold together two such impossibly separated things, times, beings, those diabolical fraternal twins 'like' and 'as' and their truly evil cousin, 'as if'. Without looking I can sense where the metaphor defeats itself. I can feel the slightly larger breasts on this girl, the more pendulous and sulky lower lip.

I have made myself impotent. This will not be believed; I will be thought a merely impotent impotent, instead of a potent one. I have willed my own impotence much as God willed His in the act of bestowing free will. A magnificent gesture. But even as I congratulate myself I feel an odd sensation; I sense an odd ambition. I am without ambition. Why, then, this urge to desert the cloister of my room when there is no need to do so, to venture into the appalling prison yard of the street?

I will not compound the damage by thinking about it. I travel blindly across the street, biting my lip. The lorries shudder through the fog, dust particles twisting in their headlights. The sly bells call.

She enters a shop. I haven't noticed the entrance before, but then I am usually preoccupied, imagining myself under the awful wheels in the road, gored and ground to powder, flung away. In the window orange neon blares DUREX. I blink at the stacks of crankery, everything from Slippery Elm Food to

Garlic Pills to Herbal Essences, brown rice, varieties of floral tea. The sign above the door reads in stark, somehow belligerent letters: HERBALIST.

It is utterly unexceptional that a hippy orphan, a waif strayed in too late from the 'sixties, should come here to be peddled natural laxatives and evil-smelling bromides. May it do her good! Another bell rings, the bell over the door, and I am within.

'May I help you?'

A curtained door behind the lady who stands coolly before me, the perpetrator of the lettering I have no doubt, and the possessor of the title it advertises, has swallowed the girl. Her part is over. I refrain from applause.

'I'd like some tea.'

She nods. A more nondescript being is not to be found. Darkish but not dark, eyes neither slanting nor sunken, an invisible person. For some reason her shallow (but not unusually so) wax-impression stiffness makes me shiver.

'Would you like something pleasant-tasting or foul?'

'Oh, foul,' I answer casually, giving as good as I get.

She nods again. 'Good!'

As she braids and unbraids the tea-leaves, concocting my brew, I wander the tiny, crowded paddock of the shop. She might be a mental defective set up in business by a compassionate relative. Or perhaps 'Herbalist' is a front for someone versed in the skills of midwifery, not above performing a quick abortion at inflated rates. Or versed in the black arts? Surely the grey arts, given her blandness? I have a strong intuition that the hippy girl behind the flowered curtain is undergoing some sort of occult or gynaecological fraud. There is some mystery here, at odds with the cluttered, nonsensical aspect of the shop, and it irks me that I cannot tease out its precise depths. I stand in an antechamber, I suspect. How to go further?

'Anything else?'

Her mental equipment is superior to mine. Of an order altogether superior to *me*. I receive this information instinctively, abruptly, and without resentment.

'Not for the moment.'

'Take it twice a day. Morning and evening. And come back to me when –'

'But I need it most in the middle of the day.'

She nods. 'Very well. Three times a day, then. But be careful. One teaspoon per cup. And come back to me when you have finished it.'

Out in the street I hug my provocative brown-paper bundle. Be careful! Even the knot in the string she has so carefully tied round it has significance. I finger the knot, I sniff the package, I concentrate on the faceless face of the Herbalist as I continue home. The route unfolds like a magic carpet beneath my feet. I make my way without pause, and am back within minutes.

I pick at the knot. Without anything having been said, it appears to me that undoing the knot is part of the ritual of the tea. I am ashamed of myself for the superstition, but I indulge it.

The tea is the greenest green I have ever seen. I am almost frightened, watching it steep. I am glad I have no mirror! What if my own face has taken on that steadily increasing green, like a season steeping in the cup? I look stealthily around the room, but it is as chalky as ever. I consume the tea. Afterwards I am exhausted and flushed, as if spring fevers really had passed into me, and I sleep.

The tea becomes my primary labour and my primary irritant. I strive to take it at the same moment each day. I place the utensils aesthetically, along Japanese lines. I never dilute it. The green becomes clearer, greener, more mesmerizing. The taste is almost non-existent, and yet I keep expecting it not so much to improve as to emerge, and I sip more and more slowly, trying to be worthy of its subtlety.

The leaves are lacklustre when I've finished, having given up their colour to the tea, and I wrap them in paper, first using the brown paper they came in, then going to the dust jackets of my books, then to the books themselves. If I had the resources to do so, I should probably bury them.

The Herbalist had given me, according to my careful measure, a week's supply of tea. Just so long I must exist before going back to her. I will not go one day early, that is the discipline, though it means missing my first cup of tea on the eighth day. I wake with the chill consciousness that I must set out before I can nurse myself awake within its green encompassing eye. The tea has been such sustenance that I have only needed, otherwise, milk, eggs, butter, bread, cheese and yoghourt, things the milkman leaves. I know the Herbalist would approve such a diet, despite its lack of greenstuffs. All that is green is provided by the tea.

I curse myself for not having gone yesterday. A tingling comes into my ears and I wonder if I am, indeed, chemically addicted, experiencing withdrawal. Then I see her! The hippy girl, trudging sullenly, as if on a reluctant errand. I fling myself after her, my pied piper, with her bells and beads, her stolen musk. Her hair twines damply, with a vinelike curl. I could reach out and pull her backwards by a trailing loop, except that I need her.

I am engorged with rage. How could I need her? I follow her to the shop. She darts inside and closes the door in my face, leaving a whiff of relief in the air, as if she knows, not only of my presence but also of my emotion. I swallow, clear my throat, enter.

'Ready for the next dose?'

Was another packet of tea to be my only reward for the week's endeavour? But I nod.

'No,' the Herbalist shakes her head. 'Not to be disappointed. Come to the back.'

The curtain sweeps us away. We stand in a room much like

the other, perhaps its twin in proportion. It seems much bigger, lacking shelves and potions. Thick green drapes fall to the floor, which is bare. A circular table faces us with a clot of drab-faced individuals seated round it. My heart sinks. I fear an anticlimax, some merely mad execution of a seance or turgid session with a ouija board.

'Be seated.'

I sit. Whatever my doubts, the Herbalist has some sort of power over me, as if I drank her will in with the tea.

'We are not here concerned with the dead,' the Herbalist's steely voice informs me. 'Do you understand?'

Nothing, I understand nothing, I want to weep with frustration. I nod. The hippy girl comes in with a tray of cups. Silence, of a different degree; the ritual has begun.

The tea is passed. The circle tenses. The girl slips into the last empty chair and sips. Communicants, we sink into the quiet. To my intense annoyance, the hippy girl starts to jabber.

'I see him,' she intones.

'I almost see him,' she qualifies.

I glare at her as she rocks blindly in her chair. Is this to be the most transparently witless of charades?

'Follow,' the Herbalist's breath blows round the table, or seems to, in a warm gust. 'Follow.'

Follow. So I had done.

'He –' she shrieks and flinches in a sharp orgasmic contraction. A second later I am shocked to hear the faintest hint of laughter in her voice. 'He was with someone,' she sighs.

There's a ripple of sympathy round the table. The Herbalist turns to me.

'It's like an electric shock,' she explains, 'when you actually discover them in the act of love. They, of course, know nothing.'

No, no, it is I who know nothing! But I nod, again, and the

Herbalist bobs her head at me in an ironic bow.

The hippy girl's voice rises. The laughter drained away, she sounds dull and worn. 'He used to talk a lot about free love,' she says. 'I thought that meant we were free to love each other.'

More sympathy emanates from behind the teacups. I look at her with loathing. Part of the unspeakable stupidity of that era. *Her* era. I sip my cool tea hastily. She converted me to it, brought me into her time. My old ways, my old gods, shuddered and fell. She made them seem more beautiful in pieces. A window is insipid, she declared. Smash it and you have a kaleidoscope. So she had crashed through my window as though it were nothing, unfrightened and unhurt, leaving only space where it had been, space and a treasure-heap of starlike, glittering glass. But they inherited light from her! When she went, only a few stuck like splinters, too deep to see or remove.

I was the keeper, the conservative. She swept away my store, my preserves, and when she swept away, too, there was nothing. I was careful, mindful of the differences between us, to leave her universe intact as I had found it, knowing it unlikely we would hold for ever. I trod carefully round her durable clichés.

They sit staring. I rub my forehead inanely and wonder, who are they? Perhaps no duller-looking than I, as they huddle in their cluster. I can't see my own features, after all; I may well be the dullard of the club, or whatever pathetic community we make up.

'Your first experience,' the Herbalist says briskly. 'An abstract experience, I believe. Yes?'

She waits. I shift on my chair and frown. What can she mean?

'You did not *see* her?'

'Her?'

'The woman you have lost. It is, I think, a woman you

67

have lost?'

'Lost?'

'Everyone here,' she indicates the others, 'has lost some-one. Not by death, but by life. Everyone here wishes – *requires* – to reassemble the lost person, much as some people require to reassemble their dead.'

'Reassemble' – like a child's toy. Yet had I not just reassembled, in the abstract, as she said, something of *her*? The – woman – I had lost? I raise my head, look at her and nod.

'Good.' There is something akin to pleasure in her voice, a distant kinship. 'Now.' She hands around packets of tea, which we grab apologetically. She accepts the grabbing, and the apology. 'That is sufficient. You will return next week.' She is not asking a question.

During the subsequent week I concentrate wholly on the tea. The green stirs more and more fully rounded memories of her, memories that make me jump up, once, twice, many more times, and leave the room. Leave the room! Leave the house, to walk or rather pound round the streets, till I come to my senses.

The hippy girl comes the following week and I pound after her, my teeth clenched.

Today one of the pale-faced speaks. There is no question of not listening with full attention.

'Oh she is – oh, she is pregnant,' he says softly. There's a long silence. Then he gets up and goes. I look at the Herbalist; her face is calm. The rest of us sit until our cups are empty and something changes in the air, the Herbalist's breath perhaps; then we go, still silent. My anger has abated.

Only to lash out virulently during the week. I jump up every day now, several times, always after the tea, and thrash around the streets. Everywhere I catch glimpses and wisps and hear bleeps of her, everywhere pursue them to a blind alley. Exhausted, I return to the Herbalist.

A whisper, the ghost of a whisper, threads its way to me, and I clutch it, pleading for more. A house begins to take shape in my mind, a house full of voices and cries of children, a house smelling unmistakably of lentils. The hippy girl starts to breathe heavily, sitting across from me in the circle, and I will her to shut up.

'Yes,' she breathes even harder. I swivel away from her in my chair, annihilating her so that I can concentrate.

'They're together,' I hear her say. I look up, impelled – she faces the Herbalist accusingly. 'You knew.'

'I suspected. But you drew one another.'

The hippy girl and I close our eyes at the same moment. *She* sweeps into view, finally. Earrings jangle at the nape of her neck, as they always did. Next into view comes the stock revolting hippy male, with bloodshot eyes and shoulder-length hair, a face beaming and repulsive.

The hippy girl convulses. Now I understand! They go down a hallway together, to a mattress on the floor of a hidden room. I can only hear, not see them. As the Herbalist promised, a bolt of sheer agony goes through me with their cries, a bolt of pure jealousy, stiffening me so that I can hardly breathe.

'Shock treatment.' I turn to the Herbalist angrily as hearing, too, fades. 'Is that it?'

She shrugs, engaged in passing out the tea.

The next week the hippy girl is gone. I raise my eyebrows and the Herbalist says crisply: 'She has finished.'

People come and go in the circle. I have brought someone here myself, as the hippy girl brought me, someone whose path crossed mine at that junction of jealousy and loss which binds the future so tightly to the past that it eradicates the present. I had forgotten the incident which bound me to the newcomer, had hardly taken it in. It occurred at a party just before she left me. So I wander past his doorway each week and wait for his footsteps behind me, hoping his anger will not be such as to overwhelm me.

THE MADNESS STORIES

The Bridge

The bridge is down.

I woke with a start like the one with which I jolted asleep. The same sense of plummeting.

Eleven thirty-three.

Thirty-three; like me.

'Thirty-three's a biggie,' said Lilian.

I didn't understand.

'Why? Thirty, okay, because you're out of the playpen of the twenties –'

'Some playpen.'

'Playpens aren't such great places to be. Thirty-five because it's midway to forty in one sense and seventy in another. Threescore and ten. But thirty-three?'

'I was thinking of Jesus,' she said sheepishly.

'Of course. How silly of me.'

Eleven thirty-five. I run a bath, flip on the kettle. Full of plans, salvaging some slim sense of morning as the morning is scuttled.

Thirty-three. Good thing I'm not a messiah. I lunge for the water expecting amniotic comfort. Blessed is the fruit of thy womb, Jesus; I always wondered what he was doing with a womb. I let out a wolverine howl.

No, that's not it. Not wolverine as in tangerine. I mean a vulpine howl. Take two, vulpine howl. The water's frigid. I forgot to switch on the immersion heater last night. Never get used to not having hot water just there, on tap, a birthright. American.

No, just childish. Never get used to not having everything on tap, a birthright. Keep wondering, where are the grown-ups? Almost miss being yelled at, except that I still am.

Stupid shit! You wanted to live on your own. You wanted to separate from that man your own father said was the best thing that ever happened to you. So he obligingly went off for a month with the kids to give you a chance to test the water.

And this is the water. Boiled away from the blackened bottom of the kettle.

Okay. Start again. Fill the kettle once more. Don't cry over boiled water.

What?

Miss Jean Brodie, wake up. You're in your prime.

I didn't mean it! Honest. It's forty. Stop blubbering. You've got seven years. Even if you've missed all the old statistical deadlines. Georgia Eliot: thirty-two before she published a line, that used to be a great comfort.

Conrad started at sixty! So he'd spent his life on the sea. So have I. Different sea. Two kids and appallingly low self-esteem.

Getting lower all the time. There's no coffee. Trudged home yesterday and fell asleep. Six p.m. Record?

Don't be modest.

Do they have tsetse flies in Greenwich? I must get some credit for spelling 'tsetse' right. Haven't seen it since my sixth-grade geography textbook.

Time flies. Time to go. At least I can walk to work. I'd jog if I put any real energy into my masochism. Flogging a dead horse.

I fought for this crummy job, against my husband and my super-ego, stenuously identified.

'This job is exactly what I need.'

'Why?'

'Because I need to be in a situation where I cannot fail. To build a little confidence.'

They sneer in unison. You? With your eduction? Your promise?

'Promise? I know what I need. A job that involves no commitment. That I can quit any time.'

The sneer becomes a glare. 'Well you do get F for commitment. F for fidelity. F –'

'Off.'

I thought the old super-e would disappear with the husband. But the latter was only an apprentice. The real thing remains.

What shall I be today? Ah, this is what you wanted a dumb job for, they sing in unison, my barbershop quartet, all razors and scissor blades flashing like legs. So you could lapse into daydream and fantasy and while away your life.

While a-waay.

It's my money I'm not making.

That shut them up. Prosperity does silence the hounds of hell, Calvin, you were quite right. Or in this case, independent poverty. I stand in peace and quiet, on the breadline.

There's the Greenwich flea market where I squander my breadline money every Saturday afternoon. Maybe I'll manage not to, today.

One pink satin bed-jacket: fifty pence.

Well, I'm practically bedridden. What the well-dressed depressive is wearing this summer. Why be a dowdy zombie? Glow in the dark, little worm.

One black skirt with orchids imprinted. One pound.

Orchids imprinted. How to resist?

If you want fungi, why not buy mushrooms? At least you could eat them.

They're aphrodisiac. Why should I add to my problems?

One black mock-leather belt to wear with the skirt. One pound fifty.

One black leotard to wear with the skirt and belt: two pounds.

An aspiring ballerina, waiting tables to put herself through the Maryinsky, and commute to Russia. Doing pliés at the bar between customers.

'Having a good stretch, dear?'

That's Verity. She owns this place. My boss. Poisonously sweet. Teeth like dainty sugar-cubes, half-sucked. Built like a doll, brittle as china. Bones are porcelain, I'm sure. Little frilly lady.

'Cup of coffee?'

Verity, my benefactor. But I still see you with a bonnet and a crook. How could you fail to recognize the dying swan in this ugly duckling?

She hands me my coffee. The first customer enters. She stifles a mad giggle behind a geisha-like hand.

'Bad luck, petal.'

I glissade to the table wearing a painful grimace. The teashop is hung with china, blue and white bone china. Verity could always get a transplant if she needed one. Blue and white checked napkins and tablecloths, white stucco walls, dolls on shelves. She used to run it as a toyshop. The Dollhouse, it's called. I'm always surprised any grown man or woman comes in here, for different reasons.

The customers are Japanese. Joy! They treat me like an empress and leave a pound on top of the service charge, which Verity pockets.

Germans treat me like an autobahn. Flatten, entering in small intimate groups of fifty. We seat thirty-five. They squeeze. Leave clean plates.

I'll leave this job racist, sexist and mercenary. Plus full of nervous tics from ducking my head and cringing to avoid the low-hanging crockery. The original bull-dyke in a china shop.

What happened to my ballerina? Where did she go? I'd much rather be her than me. Only leotards are hot. This one's stuck to me like cling-film. I can feel it encouraging fungi in my rubyfruit jungle.

I smile at the customers.

Later a religious mood descends. The walls are white stucco, Verity is a trial by fire, dreamed up by a whimsical demigod. Where's my spiritual fibre? Think of hair-shirts. Think of the discipline, think of . . .

'Afternoon, there,' booms a sailor.

What's he doing in here? Farewell, St Theresa.

She waited tables at the Blue Water Café. In an English port. Could be anywhere. Marseilles, Algeciras. She'd worked them all, slinging hash. Sometimes she forgot where she was. The men were the same.

He looked up from his heaped plate; a sailor's lunch, made up of everything Fanny cooked in the hellish little kitchen, if you could call it cooking. Poking the sausages with a pitch-fork if they protested too much. Shoving the half-charred stumps like stubbed-out cigars on to the hatch. Sausages, beans, chips. You could build skyscrapers, whole cities, out of Fanny's food.

He looked up. And he went on looking, up, his mouth working as if with laughter. There was laughter in there somewhere but it couldn't come out. At least not till he'd swallowed his food.

He was too hungry to laugh. Another mouthful followed the first, and then another. He was eating. She crossed the spaces between the tables mechanically, careful not to catch another eye. She could feel his eye on her as he chewed, insistent, possessive, watchful. A real pig. Just the way she liked them.

She stood beside his table, adding up the bill.

Like a teacher, he thought.

He asked her the time and she studied her wristwatch.

Like a nurse, taking his pulse.

'What time are you off?'

'Five.'

Plates clattered ominously in the kitchen. He stood up, digesting the information. There was no question of digesting the food.

She pocketed his tip, heard his ship hoot. Algeciras, Piraeus. They were all the same.

'Ready to close –' Verity's nose twitches anxiously. She thinks I'm in a coma.

Poor bunny. If she knew I'd turned her into a greasy gorgon. Or was that me, in the kitchen? I feel like King Kong next to Fay Wray. Maybe I should pick her up and cart her around Greenwich for a while. One hardly knows what to do, when life finally changes. And one remains lamentably the same.

I emerge with ten quid. Not bad. Has to last till Monday, mind. I will not go home past the flea market. I know my limitations.

One black net thing with blue feathers. Eight quid.

Oh, and sequins.

I walk towards the river. Stop to buy a pack of Gitanes as a vote of confidence in the future.

Huh?

Stand by the riverside, all smoke and anti-heroism. There's a boat going to Westminster. Why not? Cheaper than the flea market and more enterprising. I settle myself in the seat. The sweat begins to dry on my leotard, fanned by the breeze. I sneeze.

Always wish I'd kissed her goodnight. Mummy. Mummify her. Once the old fishmonger next door kissed her bone china neck, in her sun-dress. His father was a fishmonger, and so was he. He's coated with a layer of oil and saturated with fishy perfume. He kissed me once, too, but I couldn't get worked up enough to take offence, don't know why. Got a mouth like a fish, is that it? Suspect he is a fish. Queer fish: suspect I am? Not bad, belly thatched with tattoos like gasoline rainbows.

'Even the telly smells of fish,' his wife came in once to complain. 'Everything we watch smells of fish.'

'Where're you from?' smiles the day's second sailor.

'New Jersey,' why ruin it by adding I've been here fifteen years? He wants his American tourist, let him have her, so to speak. Why do I have to please every passing phantom?

Because.

He delivers a commentary on the riverbanks, rewarding me for my cowardice, lack of integrity, whatever. I forgot about that and all consequent lacks in my life, little items like love, money, career and sense of self, and listen to the rumours of the river instead. Each one sounds true. I believe them all. The debtors' prison with the tunnel to the pub where Shakespeare sits weeding rhymes out of his iambs and snarling 'Come over here and call it "Marlowe's Mighty Line".'

'That's Waterloo Bridge,' he says, wrapping up his discourse. 'Eighty-five per cent built by women. The only bridge that was. Leans a little to the left,' he winks as we stop, and hands me off, after asking if I'm meeting friends.

'Droves,' I murmur.

The bridge is down. I dreamed those words. I often dream in radio rather than video.

But there it is, Waterloo Bridge. Eight-five per cent female constructed. Leans a little to the left. I, too, list a little to the left and am constructed out of female matter. What's a body if not a bridge?

Where do I go from here?

I'm going to find out why women built that bridge. Meanwhile I walk. And walk. Telling myself I'm enjoying my solitary splendour. Then I stop. Why lie? I'm not enjoying it at all. I'm hating it. Why don't I just go to a lesbian bar and pick someone up?

I'm scared.

Of what?

But I've fled across the bridge at the very idea. Tomorrow morning, I've vowed to myself, I'm getting up and coming up here to the Museum of London. Maybe I'll meet someone there. Maybe it's a lesbian hangout. Why not?

I had a lover but it didn't work out. I stop on the bridge, to admire it, not to jump.

Come on, say my voices, you set it up not to work out. Why do you always fall in love with straights?

I have more in common with straights. I've led a straight life, I've got kids, I . . .

What's having in common got to do with it? What have you got to learn from them about how to live your life?

The bridge feels safe as houses. Sturdy, plunging down to the bottom of the river, rising up smooth and curved, listing a little to the left. By the time I get home it's all of seven o'clock. I manage to stay conscious till eight.

Ha, ha, Sunday. The Salvation Army blares me awake. So much for all those sweet lesbian schoolteachers at the Museum of London.

Onward, Christian Soldiers. They toot on up the street. There's still no coffee. I get up, switch on the hot water, heave myself back to bed. Bridges swing through my dreams, all loose, painful as hang-nails, broken bones, unset. Splintering music. Bridges built of wood, not stone like the massive Waterloo. Built by women, I remind myself, waking fitfully. Must find out why. Always had a thing about bridges. Loved them, as a child. The George Washington, the Tappan Zee. Then. When? Lost my nerve. Bridges folded up. Rivers gaped. I set foot on a bridge and it swings loose from its moorings on the other side. Turn around, start to walk back where I came from; a creak warns me not to attempt it. Stand. Still. It'll fall off its hinges anyway and drift away with me like an eskimo on an ice-floe, into forever. Wake up.

Hot water. Rain. Force myself out, using coffee as a sort of crowbar. Wander, looking for a shop on the Lee High Road. Chat with the Pakistani woman in the shop and that's a gap bridged. Only takes a word, only a face, only a smile. Why then do I stay away, locked inside? Why indeed. Take the newspapers and coffee home. Burst into tears as soon as the door closes, disappointed child.

Read paper, drink coffee, it'd be a virtue to venture out to the Off Licence but I can't be bothered, that's a vice. Would rather curl up and fall asleep. Rain inside and out. Tomorrow: the moon's day. Made it to the museum. No nice teachers but some little hints, titbits of information, piecemeal history. Old bridge collapsed 1934. Cornerstone for new laid 1939. Finished 1944.

That's why women built it. Children stream past me, their voices echo as if we were all in a swimming pool. War work. Not that it's recorded or remembered, except by the sailor who told me.

Back to the Dollhouse. I walk across the bridge again. Getting to be a sort of pilgrimage. It's firm. Concrete pillars sunk into the tide. I shall come back tonight. Why? Because this is, suddenly, where I have to be.

Because there's a For Sale sign on my house, on my life?

Because my bridges are washed out. I need to take lessons in bridge-building.

Maybe my leanings towards the left, brain sinister, are methods, not symptoms, of madness.

I don't believe it for a moment. The Dollhouse door opens and I shrink inside.

An old tramp comes in. I almost whisper to him to go away, please, he won't meet kindness here. But I don't, I take him a menu over Verity's frown. He orders tea. His hand shakes so much he spills tea on the blue and white checks. And then tobacco on top of it when he rolls himself a cigarette. Of course he stays all afternoon. It's his shelter, and our tea's expensive. I ignore Verity's nudges, polish the dolls on the shelves, washing their little faces with the cloth.

She signals me unequivocally to her side. When I get there she draws me by the elbow behind the counter and shows me the knives arranged, waiting, inclining her head in grotesque semaphore towards the tramp.

I stare at her. Why am I worried about craziness?

When he shambles out, having paid, she's embarrassed. Takes it out on me, making me hoover the upstairs, wash down the tables. I almost feel sorry for her.

Outside, turn towards the river in a light rain. No sailors. Today's theme is tramps, dereliction; why do I suffer from mild agoraphobia? Afraid if I ever got going I'd never get back. Home. Wander for ever. What they call a fugue state. Going nowhere, or everywhere. There is someone in me who could wander for ever, for love of the world. The best, maybe the only way, to see it, hold, cherish it.

But if you refuse to specify or specialize your love, after a while it thins and you lose the lot. Don't know why. Like you have to have a place to retire and rest from your wanderings or they become tinged with bitterness, then corroded. You must rest and must have a return on your interest, curiosity, love; or they wane, they wane.

Is that the fear? That the mad and incipiently bitter person gets out and takes over? She must be caged in a house, must be kept on a leash. The one who talks to herself all the time; aloud. The more so, the less I put down on the white bridge of paper. Until she expects no answer; every answer's an insult, every response from the world an assault.

But then – maybe the writers who sit in cafés scribbling have found a Buddhist middle way between the garret and the street. But do you have to be born to it? Or coddled in a special city? People don't like it if you pull our pens and pencils here. I can imagine Verity, if anyone tried it! Come after them with a carving knife.

There are stations, department stores. Uninviting, cold, but tolerant.

I shamble off the boat, walk. Walk. Call somebody?

Don't know anybody to call, any more. Between two lives. Between incarnations. What bridges the gap? Picked the phone up last night. Listened; its pulse was normal. Put it down again. A bridge of sorts. But I don't use it. There's no one I can talk to without mortgaging something. I'm already mortgaged to the hilt.

And if I did take out another? Invitation for dinner, nostalgia for what I don't want. Nothing comes easier. Need nostalgia like herpes. Less.

Had nostalgia for years. Nostalgia for convent school. Why? Because that was the last time I could be innocently gay and innocently crazy and innocently enjoy both. The crazed mind, the sapphic intensity.

Listen to nostalgia. It says: I want to be there. It means: I don't want to be here. It says: yesterday was heaven. It means: today is hell.

I know all that.

Good, good! So it wasn't all a waste.

I go home and fall asleep in front of a crappy TV programme nostalgically listening to the American accents.

Nostalgia says: I miss these accents.

Nostalgia means: it's much too quiet around here.

Awakened by the phone. Everything's coming up roses till Verity says, in a lapdog's sharp bark: 'Are you coming in, Petal?'

Petal gets up. In a giving of rotten old timbers recalled

from a dream, a snapping of beams like the logs in a fire. Lot of destruction going on these nights, no wonder I'm so tired all day.

Yawn through a mercifully quiet day. Stalk down to the river. Sit by the riverbank, empty of thought. A vegetative day. All right; they happen.

That bridge was built by women. It took years. Not days not weeks not months. Years. Some of them probably scared to come out of their cosiness after all that time. Coaxed by necessity, not like you, by freedom's sweet scary wind.

The bridge is down. All my bridges. Burnt, snapped, washed away. Time to build. But not in a day.

I can't wait.

Who said wait?

I walk, anxious, fending off pain. Stop on the bridge and let it cascade like a shower inside, like thunderous tropical rain till it leaks out of the portholes. Something happens. They turn on blue loops of light like a sash across the river's belly. Graceful blue half-moons. The book in the museum did say it was London's most graceful bridge.

This summer's, this moment's, a bridge. The only kind you'll ever get's the kind you build. Not the most graceful arabesque of a bridge. Makeshift, sometimes. But they get you across. The present's no more than that, a bridge over a canyon, a roaring river, between two shores, one fading, one approaching. Space has changed, the world's shrunk, some-one said, and I said no, only time's expanded because we live so much longer.

Why did I think of that?

You've put down a cornerstone. Made a start. Stop looking to see if it's all done perfectly, and get going. Walk and mutter all you like, see what develops. Who.

I drift into Waterloo Station, buy a notebook. Get on the train clutching it foolishly. Cardinal rule: don't be afraid to be foolish.

I can see the blue ribbon, blue for first prize, like a decoration for bravery. There's all kinds.

Some of them must've been secretly relieved when they were herded home again, after the war. Could indulge in some secret nostalgia now and then.

But the bridge remains. Trouble is you have to keep the thing in good repair. Crawl around inspecting it. Laughing. Wonder if anyone swayed, vertiginous, wanting to jump? Of course she did.

They built. And built. According to a secret recipe: they lean, a little to the left.

That's a very little bit better.-

Cassandra

Section of the interhemispheric tracts (commissurotomy) to control epilepsy has been found to eliminate much of the normal integration of sensory information . . . For instance commissurotomized subjects cannot put words to music, or music to words. Subjects could identify by pointing to stimuli seen in the left-field and by naming stimuli simultaneously seen in the right field. They could not explain the discrepancy and they gave no indication that they had seen either stimulus as other than complete and regular. The recognition and memory of faces – a skill of the 'minor' (right) hemisphere – cannot be articulated in language – a skill of the 'major' (left) hemisphere. Catastrophic reactions and feelings of guilt and depression were common after left-hemisphere anaesthetization; while feelings of euphoria often followed right-side anaesthetization. Commissurotomized patients reacted strongly with blushing and giggling to the presentation of pictures of nudes in the left visual field, even when the 'major' hemisphere showed by its verbalizations that it had no idea why this was happening. The right hemisphere outperformed the left in accurate perception and memory of stimuli that have no verbal label or are too complex or too similar to express the words, but only the left hemisphere can give language to these memories.

There is a gap and she knows there is a gap between what she sees and what she says. She cannot, she cannot leap the gap. It is lonely. It is cold. There are too many feelings of depression and guilt and euphoria. She feels entirely alone, and the horizon still glows with the burning of the towers of Ilium.

The severing of the *corpus callosum*, the hard bond of nerves that connects the left and right hemispheres of the brain, has been found to eliminate the normal integration of sensory information.

He watches her unhappily as she stands in the prow of the boat; she looks huddled and cold. The usual scars, bruises and scratches on her face seem to stand out. She seems small and frail. Her beauty is not diminished, indeed it is undeniable, overwhelming, but suddenly it is the beauty of a child, not of a woman. A child, and a sad lost child at that. He draws in a breath, racked with a new pain. He, Agamemnon, King of Argos, commander of the victorious forces of Greece, is in pain; and the pain is inflicted on him by a little hunched child who rides the prow of his boat with an unreadable expression. It is called compassion, that is the name of his pain, and he is not used to feeling it. They say, the Greek warriors, that he struck a poor bargain in the taking of the spoils; that he chose the mad woman, the crazy one, when he could have chosen the voluptuous courtesans of Troy, any of the women of the city who flocked in defeat about his feet and begged to be his portion. He knows, fretfully, that he made the best bargain of his life, that just to have her, have her here, untouchable and untouched, to have her ride the prow of his ship and gaze at the sea with her dark eyes, that this is enough. And if he is gentle, gentle and patient as a fisherman, strong and unmoving as the sea, she will come to him and tell him, tell him what it is, what happens in her head, what happened in the beginning to make her so different from other women, so alone, so powerful, so frail. But the pain of patience irks him and he paces the boat half-irritated.

He is wrong. She will not tell him. She will not tell him any of it. At one moment she is riding the ship, mourning the city of her childhood, mourning the bright princes who were her brothers, mourning the gallant stupidity with which they died. 'Hector,' she murmurs, but even as she says his name his face disappears from her mind, and when she finds the face again she does not know whose face it is. She likes Agamemnon. She has a knowing that he will not . . . that he will wait . . . that he will . . . she does not know the word for what it is she fears, for what it is she knows he will not do. Then the next minute it is gone, it is all gone; there is a clear, familiar, strange sensation which begins in the middle finger of her left hand and spreads through her body, a feeling of intense stillness and power that reaches out from inside her to the whole sea; and the bright islands of the Aegean dance on the water, totally vital, totally still. A transparent moment, turning from gold to green. Everything is green. Green. She feels quite clearly the spittle forming on her lips, she hears her own mouth open with a strange birdlike noise, she feels her whole body lurch forward, her shoulders smashing down, the heel of the God forcing her face into the wooden deck.

He runs along the ship, suddenly shaken into movement. He feels immediately the compassion of the crew, but his fear is that she will fall into the sea. He forces her mouth open, inserts the leather scabbard of his dagger between her teeth, wipes the foam from the side of her mouth, tries to hold her firmly but gently, and is amazed at the extraordinary strength of her convulsions. It does not last long; as suddenly as it started she flops against him, limp, washed out like a soft cloth. She opens her eyes and smiles at him.

'She will kill you,' she says, 'in water. Not in the sea, which can wash away the blood. She will kill you. There will be a lot of blood. I can see it.'

'It's all right,' he says, 'it's all right, don't worry. I'm here, I won't let anyone hurt you.'

'Not me. You. It's the swan's eggs; there was too much blood, there in the laying of the eggs, too much blood and yours will be there.'

'Don't worry,' he says again desperately. Is the look in her eyes consent or despair? Quite suddenly she seems very sleepy. He gathers her up in his arms and carries her like a little child below decks and there on his own bunk, surrounded by the outward signs of his military prestige – sword, helmet, trophies from Troy – she sleeps, curled round; the scab of blood on her lip looking like the traces of a child's sweetmeat. She seems innocent and open, but she is closed off from him. Asleep, this feels forgivable, although with a sigh he knows he would forgive her anyway. He tries to focus on what she said. He had killed his own daughter for a prophecy; he believes in prophecy. 'She will kill you.' The first time she had said it it had been with urgency, with commitment. It was only the repetition that had sounded crazed. As he tries to concentrate he sees the speckled foam from her mouth still clinging to his left sleeve, he remembers the power of her body racked by the convulsions. She was raving. He shrugs his shoulders. Of course she was raving, he tells himself. Standing up he feels his tunic wet against his stomach. She had lost control of her bladder and he had carried her closely: he does not know why he is touched instead of revolted. Checking surreptitiously that she is truly asleep he strips and changes. He wants to promise the world to her; he wants, against his own self-knowledge, to swear that he will never use his power against her, that he will keep her safe, that he will never do anything she does not like. But she is asleep, uninterested in his professions, in his promises.

She dreams. But even she does not know what she dreams.

Troy burns. The flames are high and hot. She has fled from the broken city to a sanctuary. But the Greeks come there and all women are spoils of war. She is spoiled, despoiled, raped. There is no end to it; the flames in her eyes and in her belly. Her vagina broken, the secret places smashed into. She could have suffered this in the beginning, and then all would have been well.

Hector's body is dragged around the walls of the city. She sees Helen smile faintly, uncaring. She sees the eyes of Paris, her favourite brother, light up with jealousy relieved. Paris has hated Hector for years. Hector, the bravest of the Trojans, the hero without blemish, is dragged round the walls of Troy and her sad old father has to beg his enemies for the return of the battered flesh.

Agamemnon who has rescued her is chopped up with an axe. Undignified, struggling to pull on a tunic whose arm-holes have been sewn together. An infantile prank turned deadly. And everything she sees, she sees over and over and over again. Again and again in the still, pure moment before the God stamps on her shoulders and flattens her to the ground, she sees. She sees what will happen and she tells it and no one can believe her. She cannot believe herself; in each bitter instant Cassandra hears her own truths as spittle and crazed foaming. There is a gap and she knows there is a gap between what she sees and what she says. She cannot, she cannot leap that gap. She cannot fit the words to music, nor music to words. She cannot remember faces and names at the same time. It is very lonely.

Commissurotomy – the severing of the *corpus callosum*, the tissue which provides the connection between the two functionally asymmetric hemispheres of the brain – has been found to eliminate the normal integration of sensory information. The left hemisphere thus receives detailed information about visual stimuli only if they fall in the right visual half-field and about some asthetic stimuli only if they contact the right side of the body. The same is obviously true for the right hemisphere. The two hemispheres process information differently; the left hemisphere being superior in terms of language function while the right is superior when required to perform a spatial transformation on sensory input. Moreover there is competition between the left and right hemispheres of commissurotomized patients for control of motor output; and this leads to further, complicated distortions in motor-dependent communication.

She is a very beautiful woman. No one ever questioned this, even with the inevitable cuts and bruises to her face and hands; and her frequently bizarre and inappropriate expressions. She had been, though, a radiant child. Loving, laughing, lovely. Cassandra. Now there is, inside her own ears, a hissing and a writhing in her name; but then there had been a musical giggle.

Apollo had desired her. No, Apollo had loved her. But this she does not remember. She remembers nothing about this at all. It is all burned away. She sees the future, but she does not see the past. She does not remember, recall, recollect.

But Apollo, the burning sun-god, the most beautiful, most vital of the Olympians, loved her. Before there was time for confusion, before there was time for anyone else, he came to her. Just post-menarche, still joyful in her own power, still untried, untouched. Too much love for one so simple. His desire left him insensitive to his love. He would not be stayed. The horses of the sun champed on their bits while he spoke with her; she was blinded, confused by his brightness. Perhaps she did not even know what he was talking about. It was the first time. The first time that every inch of her flesh reached out greedy, greedy and needy. There was no past, no future; no family, no friends. He offered her anything, anything that she wanted; he was a god and his godliness rose up between his legs just to watch her considering the offer, halfway between greedy spoiled child and greedy sexy woman. He felt his power and prepared to produce for her castles made of ice that would not melt although the sun shone day and night upon them. He prepared to unsling his own lute from his shoulders and give her authority over all the music in the world. He prepared to summon Pegasus so that she might ride on the great winged horse and bestride the mountains and the oceans to the stabling place of the golden sun chariot and the eight great stallions that pulled it. His power to give her what she wanted delighted him. And she asked him for a spiral shell that was pink inside and without a chip missing. She and her sisters had a collection of shells; they would walk with their handmaids beside the sea and gather up beautiful shells from the beautiful beaches of Ilium and carry them home; but none of them had ever found an unflawed, perfect, spiralled horn with the silvery pink lining. The request struck his pride, and in his anger he laughed at her and she was humiliated. She spoke as a child and was exposed as a child, and in the shadow of his mockery she became a woman, a woman who knew her power over men and gods. She said, 'Give me the power to tell the future, give me the power to know what will happen. Make me a prophetess and a seer and a soothsayer and an oracle. If you can.'

There was a flicker, a flicker in the sunlight by the river. There are things that are not permitted, even to the most golden and potent of young gods. The sunlight flickered, and the flickering was the shadow of his doubt. She sat, not caring, as happy to dabble her toes in the river and smile as she was to be given this thing. But she clearly sensed her own desirability, and she pulled in her cheeks and pouted and looked little and cross and his heart melted with . . . with what? with lust, with amusement, with tenderness, with the desire to show off? She was old enough to seduce and not old enough to know what it meant. He knew then that he did not have the right; that he could give her presents and affection, and love, but he did not have the right to take her, to own her, to possess her whole lovely sweet virginal body. And he was ashamed, and angry and greedy. So he did not restrain himself from using all his power.

'If I do that for you what will you do for me?'

'What do you want?'

She became sly, the slyness of curiosity, because she wanted to know, wanted to know what this feeling was, both the feeling of power and the feeling of reaching towards, wanting, wanting, wanting.

'I want you to be my lover.'

She laughed. It seemed so little a thing, of course she would love someone who gave her what she wanted; and the words brought a feeling to her arms and her high hard little breasts; the tickling rising feeling in her nipples and the soft sinking feeling in the pit of her belly, and she wanted suddenly to cover his golden body with honey all over and lick it off slowly, slowly in the sunshine. She wanted to spread her legs and . . . and she knew not what, but she consented to the bargain.

And now he was haughty and calm. He spat neatly on his finger, and crouched down beside her on the grass. He touched quite gently her lips, and then her eyes, and last her ears, and when he touched her ears she saw the first high flames leap above the topless towers of Troy and felt the great grief of loss and pain and the great chasm of fear, but before she could think about it he took his finger and laid it on her right nipple and the darkness vanished and she reached up with the innocence of a child and the passion of a woman and put her arms around him and gave his neck a long kiss. They stayed there a minute and her desire mounted. Then he took his hand away from her breast and placed it under her chin and compelled her mouth towards his. The sun shone and she was full of joy and curiosity and excitement.

Then he kissed her.

She responded to his kiss with an eagerness, a voluptuous enthusiasm, receiving his tongue deep in her mouth and working her own with happy little wriggles along the inside of his lip. And he pushed her gently backwards and kissed her deeper, harder, more demandingly, reaching with his free hand for her white thigh. And suddenly she could not.

It was too much, too much feeling, too much closeness, there was no Cassandra, no princess there, but only flesh and burning flesh and she could not. She was frightened. He did not feel her fear, he could not give her space, he was not willing to wait. She pushed at him and there was no escape, and she hit out at his face with her hands, and she bent her head back strangely and banged it, banged it on a rock. She was outside herself and unable to think, unable to breathe, and there was too much feeling and he was too close and she would not survive it, and she could not bear it, and she could not, she could not, she could not. Her whole self went cold, because it was too much. Too much feeling, and she would be lost in it, lost if she let him nearer to her own darkness and let him illuminate it with light. And she beat at him and herself, fluttering like a bird, not like a little chicken bird but like a trapped eagle.

'I can't,' she cried. 'Stop it, let me go. I can't.'

'You must,' he said. 'You like it.'

'I know. Yes. No. No I don't like it. I won't. I can't.' And she scratched at him, and at herself, her nails tearing her own face and his. He thought at first it was her passion and he was excited, but she beat and fought, lost, lost, lost, in a strange place and insanely she muttered and banged and struggled.

95

He could not speak to her, she had gone away. He was almost frightened, but more angry. He could not for some time get her back to him, get her conscious. She was shaking and deranged. She was mute and broken.

'You have to,' he said, 'you promised. We made a bargain.'

'I don't care. I cannot.' Now she was sulking like a baby, her face turned away. She knew only that it would kill her if she did, that the explosion in her would kill her if she let him bring that golden pleasure any nearer. He could kill her by some other means if he wanted to, she was not going there. She was shaking with fear.

'I don't want it. I don't want your present. I don't want to know the future. I was only joking.'

He has made love to mortals before and they have delighted in him; who is she, this child, to make mock of a god's desire? Who is she to shame him and despise him? And seeing her as a child, he is more ashamed than ever. And like white heat his anger rises, rises to replace the rising of his genitals which are withered by her rejection.

'We gods don't take back our gifts. But I will punish you.'

'Yes,' she sighs, 'yes, do that.' The punishment will obliterate the dangerous joy; she will not go to that perilous place, the punishment will take away the memory of the pleasure. 'Please.'

He is vengeful because he is baffled and embarrassed. He is vengeful because he is ashamed. She does not look radiant now, but little and shrivelled.

'I won't take back my gift,' he tells her, 'but I shall make it so that you will always know the future but no credit or reliance will ever be placed on anything you say. Ever. Even by you. Since you make a gap between me and my desire I shall make one between your seeing and your saying. You can never leap that gap. You will never leap that gap. It will be a very lonely place.'

He stood her up. He held her by the shoulders and he

looked at her. She felt the desire rise again and with it the fear. The desire, the fear, the pain. She cannot. But now he does not let her go. His hands are very hard; they shift from her shoulders to her upper arms, which he grips tightly.

'You're hurting me,' she says, trying to wriggle free.

'I know,' he says, without compassion. He puts his tongue on her lips, but now there is no desire, his tongue is like a knife, he runs it up the narrow crevice above her upper lip, very slowly, very coldly. She feels his saliva on her like a snail's trail; straight up the middle of her nose and forehead. With the force of his chin he bows her head and runs his hard cutting tongue right across the centre of her crown, and she feels the sharp blade cut into her cranium, and into the depths of her brain, a single even slicing and there is intolerable pain, intolerable confusion. Her mind is severed. She is severed. There is a gap between her seeing and her saying. It is a very lonely place. It is very cold. The words and the music separate: she feels them pulling apart, stretching out, out, till the song collapses into chaos and she will never sing again. She feels catastrophic reactions of guilt and depression and euphoria. She remembers faces and names but she cannot associate them with each other. The normal integration of sensory knowledge is destroyed. She faints.

When she becomes conscious, she does not remember. They do not understand the long scratches on her face, nor the bruising on her head until she starts having fits. In her fits she murmurs dreadful and dangerous things, lost perceptions that make no sense but are discouraging and not to be encouraged. Although she is very beautiful they conclude that she is mad. She is often placed under restraint, because of the complicated distortions in all her forms of communication. She likes men still, but she will not let anyone touch her. She will never let anyone touch her although she is not able to say why.

She says over and over again that Troy will be destroyed.

The city will burn, she tells them. The flames will be high and bright. As bright as a god, she says. But she also says as bright as lentils, or as bright as three days ago, or as bright as stag's antlers so they do not understand. They place no credit or reliance on anything she ever says, and she does not know why.

When she wakes up in Agamemnon's bunk she does not remember what has happened. He comes down again into the cabin and smiles at her. She smiles back, warm and sleepy. He is overwhelmed again with tenderness. He will not hurry, he must not hurry, he will be patient, patient and kind, because she moves him so, as no woman has ever done.

'Feeling better?' He fills the hatchway and for a moment cuts off the light. They rock together in the dark movement of the ship's belly.

'I feel fine,' she replies, then as he moves the light floods back into the small space, she smiles radiantly and says, 'She'll kill you. With an axe. So don't change your tunic. In the bath.'

He thinks it is a joke; that perhaps she was awake when he changed his tunic before, and is teasing him.

'All right,' he says, 'that's all right.'

'I know,' she says, giggling because his smile in the half-light is so sweet. 'By the way, she'll kill me too.' They both laugh and the ship sails gently on towards Argos and Clytemnestra who will indeed kill both of them.

Despite its effectiveness in the control of certain forms of epilepsy, commissurotomy (section of the *corpus callosum* – the interhemispheric tract) is no longer used as a surgical treatment. Since the discovery of multiple functional asymmetries favouring the right as well as the left hemisphere, it is generally recognized that the therapeutic value of this intervention is outweighed by the fact that it has been found to eliminate much of the normal integration of sensory information.

The information on hemispheric section comes principally from Robert Nebes's article in Marcel Kinsbourbe (ed.) *Asymmetrical Function of the Brain* (Cambridge University Press, 1978), to whom thanks.

THE BIRTH STORIES

Forceps Delivery

None may presume her faith to prove
He proffers death that proffers love.
    Edmund Waller, 'On the Marriage of the Dwarfs'

Date: 1670
Place: Paris, the Salle St-Joseph, the lying-in ward of the Hôtel Dieu, the Parisian charity hospital founded in A.D. 641 by St Landry, Bishop of Paris; and the adjoining delivery-room, the Chauffroy, so called because a fire was kept burning there to warm the mothers and neo-natal children.
Cast: *Dr Hugh Chamberlen* – a member of an eminent and hugely successful family of obstetricians. His grandfather and great-uncle, Huguenot refugees to England in the late sixteenth century, had invented the obstetric forceps, and the family had kept this as their well-advertised family 'secret' for a century, to their immense profit and prestige, despite their own explicit recognition that a more general knowledge would save the lives of thousands of mothers and children during this period – before the discovery of asepsis and safer Caesarian section. (Without the forceps, in the event of a fully obstructed labour the choice was to let the mother labour until her uterus ruptured and she died, or to chop up the child

in utero, smashing its skull and then removing it piecemeal with hooks; this often entailed very serious damage to the mother, particularly as modesty and the law demanded that the obstetrician should keep the woman's body covered, and so invisible, at all times.) In 1670, aged forty, Dr Chamberlen went to France and offered his family secret for sale to *Dr François Mariceau*, who although only thirty-three was recognized as the leading obstetrician in Europe. In 1668 he had published his *Observations sur le Grossesse et l'Accouchement* which became the authoritative text-book on the subject for many years. (Dr Hugh Chamberlen, after his return from France, published the English translation of this work.) Dr Mariceau was not eager to pay the fabulous sum proposed for an unspecified product and proposed a test case. He had in his care a *severely deformed rachitic dwarf primipara* aged twenty-eight and nameless. After examining her he concluded that the case was impossible; if Dr Chamberlen could deliver her the secret would be worth paying for.

Now read on.

There are too many rhythms. Too many rhythms. I cannot settle into the pattern of a rhythm because of the others. Now I am gone into the place of infinite darkness, the place of impossible slavery, the labour for the child who cannot be born, I find too many rhythms.

Four days ago my waters broke. But the pains did not come. They walked me. They walked and jolted and jumped and shook me for three days and three nights. They came, the nurses came. They broke into my silence. They said, 'Put your arms around our shoulders and we will walk you. Up and down. Up and down.' Up and down. So that is the first rhythm. The rhythm of the walking. One two, one two, one two. Left right, left right. Up. Down. It is not easy to walk a dwarf. I know that. But it is not easy to be a dwarf. They walked me in shifts. Some were kind. Some were efficient, which is better than kind, for me. But some, when their shoulders ached, or their backs were tired and lop-sided, they would straighten a little and then my feet do not reach the ground. My feet would trail, dragged behind. They would hang down, heavy feet on ugly bent legs, toes scuffling along the floor as I try to walk. Up and down. Up and down. One two. One two. Heavy, implacable, useless. The Princess had to sort the seeds, all the mixed seeds had to be sorted. Impossible task. Impossible useless task. But the birds came. The birds helped her. Nature came to her aid. But not to mine. Because I am unnatural. There is only the beat of the impossible walking. Stomp. Stomp. Stomp. It does not go away, even now, even at the end.

After three days of that stomping they changed their minds. They gave me a massive dose of senna and laid me down. And at first it seemed a sweet relief. To lie there on the bed alone and let go. Let it all go, rich and warm and stinking, flowing and farting, letting go as though the baby could be born that way, just letting go and sliding out. But then afterwards the pains came and I had not known. And that is the second rhythm, the rhythm of the pains. They come, they come from outside and from inside, in waves almost elegant, so total, so demanding, so absolute. They start far away, low and musical, and the flow upwards rising, rising higher and higher above my head and they sweep up and up to a crest that will finally swallow me altogether and there will be no other place and then, there, high above the world in a moment of perfected purity, perfected intensity, there at the moment of annihilation there is the turning, the retreat, the long harsh undertow of defeat. There at the riding point, there in the promise that everything will be simplified down into pure bright colours – red, green, yellow – there is the turning, the declining, the moving away. And down in the trough in the quiet space which the pain has created there is the moment of perfect repose, the knowledge of eternity and the fear of hell and the sight of heaven. There is a sense that the pain is pushing, pushing me down further down and lower on the bed; and I am longing, longing for someone to come, longing that they will come and lift me up, strong hands under my arm-pits to lift me up to a position where I can meet the pain in all its power, meet it fair and square. Exausted by the flawless pain, pinned by it, flattened, swept away into its depth, I desire that someone else should be here, someone else to come and lift me up, up, up against that rhythm, so as to greet it as a friend, and no one comes. And struggling to find someone, some place, some space, some height, some elevation in the calm moment at the bottom of the trough of pain, the great wave comes again too soon, just too soon, just as I know I could find a way to be ready and eager, it comes too soon. And that rhythm goes on and on, like at the seashore, where you can watch all day and there is change but no ending, no break, no moment of stillness, but only the rising and falling, rising and falling, rising and falling of the waves that come from far away, from beyond the horizon. Out there, beyond where the sun sinks, is where the waves come from and there is hypnotic movement, where one longs for stillness and longs not to have one's longing met. And I know that the waves are not my own, not mine alone, but like the waves of the sea are universal and belong to all the women who come to this place, to this beaching point and stand looking out towards the New World, where nothing will ever be the same again. And at this point I can, almost, almost, enter into and enjoy the rhythm of it, because it joins me to all the women, all the mothers, whom I am not like and whom I can never be like, except here in the grip of the waves of pain. Almost. But also there is no escaping from the pain, so it must be lived with.

These things I learn here, flattened on this bed. I learn them and know them in the great swelling and ebbing of the rhythm of the pain. I know them and I tell them to myself and there is no comfort. But I do not complain, I do not cry out, I do not ask for any relief, because it is not consonant with my dignity to do so, and I have so little dignity. I have come to a place, the end of a nine-month journey, where I will abide in silence; where I will curl up in the silence of my pain and endure, endure, endure, for the victim of achondroplasia is a silent bear. I retreat, I retreat deep, deep into my lair, hibernating myself from it all, and I seek in silence the depths of the cave of pain, the belly of it where the child that is me and the child that is in me, both, still, against the impossible odds, struggle for survival.

But they will not leave me in my lair. They will not let me be. There is another movement, a different rhythm and it is none of my making and it is intruded upon me. I search for a poised place, a balance, a harmony between the rhythm of the stomping and the rhythm of the pain, contrapuntal, like singing a round, both parts, oneself. And as I glimpse, pursue the idea of a pattern here, it is broken in upon, shattered, fragmented, by the comings and goings of the two doctors, and the game they are playing together.

Dr Hugh Chamberlen is forty years old. He is a large and flamboyant man, with red hair and huge hands. He is famous. He is a famous obstetrician. He has, they say, astonishing success in a large number of difficult cases in his native London. He is obstetrician to the royal court, but his fame is not based on this alone. His family have been famous obstetricians for a century. They have a secret, they are not secret about this, it is well known and much vaunted. But no one knows what it is. His family are called in when all goes awry at the labours of the richest in the land. They arrive with a huge strange chest. It is carried into the room where the woman is in labour. Everyone else is sent out. The woman herself is blindfolded. Dr Chamberlen's hands reach under the sheet. He smiles with confidence. His strong and hearty voice tells her all will be well. She can hear him muttering, feel him digging into her, and then she can feel the child moving. Where it had refused to move, it moves, it moves down the birth canal and is born.

When he came first I was encouraged. He seemed so full of confidence, this flashy and fashionable man. No problem, he says, no problem. The secret enables me to deliver in a matter of minutes the most difficult of cases. Fifteen mins max. in your case, he says with a smile. Suddenly I do not trust him. He cares not about my pain, but about his triumph. And his triumph is not over the difficult delivery, it is over Dr François Mariceau. Dr Mariceau. I thought he was a lovely man, Dr Mariceau. He seemed interested in me. He is thirty-three. He is tiny. He has tiny soft hands. He is the doctor here. They call him 'the Oracle' because he knows so much about the delivery of babies and writes wise books. So. I liked his gentle hands. But I see the two of them smile at each other. They are playing a game and it has nothing to do with me. Over the hours the game is intruded into me, like the secret. Dr Chamberlen wants to sell his secret to Dr Mariceau. He wants a lot of money, ten thousand *livres* they say. Dr Mariceau is canny. He does not want to spend all this money on a duff deal, he wants an authentic demonstration. He examines me, with his students. I will do nicely. The foetal head, they mutter, is too high, disengaged – and am I disengaged from this conversation, I am supposed to be. The baby has its face pressed to my belly. I did not know until then that it should not have, it should be backwards, pressed towards my buttocks; I wonder if the effects of the senna repelled it, made it turn around. There are things you do not ask doctors. Clearly, they agreed, the case was impossible. Let Dr Chamberlen try his secret; if it works on me it's worth the price.

You see their rhythm imposes itself on mine. I too become rational, worldly, slightly jaundiced, hearing them. I cannot fly back into my silence and my weighted waiting. Not in their presence.

They like each other, these two. I realize that. It is a game they are playing, a game with some pride and some money invested, but a game nonetheless and played between friends who respect each other. I would like to play too, I would. I think I could hold a strong hand in this game, but then it would not be between friends. It does not matter who wins this expensive game. It will not be me. It will not be me.

So they walk me and dose me and walk me and the pains move me and lift me, and they ignore the pains and do not wait for the rhythm of them. They prod me and feel me. Their game is graceful and fun for them, and I am not part of it. They take me into the Chauffroy and it is warm and I would like to sleep there, but there is no resting among the conflicting, tugging rhythms. Dr Mariceau is laughing, smiling, as he leaves; should he go to the bank, he asks, to get the ten thousand *livres*; and Dr Chamberlen laughs too and says there will not be time because he will in minutes deliver me of a fine son. I want to tell him that I will die, I will not have a child at all, but that if I do I want a daughter, but then I will have broken my silence and will have no more defences against them. Silence is hard earned, hard bought, it cannot be sold as cheaply as this big man's secret. I have fought for mine and won it, and it does not matter if he wants to deliver me of a fine son.

He is jovial, this English doctor. He cannot even talk to me in my own language, he does not even try. There is no one in the room but him and me, so that the secret can be preserved. His hands are too big. They have no respect for the other rhythms. They are too huge. He feels me. His fingers seek out my dark and secret places. His hands plunge in. And I know, suddenly and with agony, that first he wants to make a lot of money; but secondly his power and my deformity, his power over my body, which he cannot see because it is covered, his hands reaching and groping; he cannot forgive

109

me for his curiosity; he cannot forgive me for making him curious, making him excited, even making him rich. I have experienced this before, the power of excitement that my strange, ugly, hated body has, and the power of the guilt and anger and unforgiveness. But before I could always walk away. And now I cannot walk away.

His hands withdraw. He will be without mercy now, only full of pride and determination. From his bag he takes the secret. He knows of his own failure now because he does not blindfold me. He makes no attempt to keep the secret from me. Or perhaps because I am silent, always silent, silent and deformed, he thinks I cannot talk, thinks I am stupid and ignorant. He puts his secret claws into my flesh; reaching in; hard, cold and going in.

I do not think of the child.

I never think of the child in there.

I will not think about the child that is trapped in there.

Trapped in my body as I am trapped in my body.

I refuse to think of the child, for fear that I might love it.

I never think of the child in there.

For three hours he works on me. It is arhythmic.

Dr Mariceau admires his efforts. Once he pauses to regain his breath. The tugging and the pushing. Getting the baby out is like getting the baby in. So much effort for the poor man. Ha. He is sweating. I am sweating too but that is different. With the sheet covering the secret, covering me too, though that seems not so important to him, he lets Mariceau enter.

The head is engaged now, he says, but the pubic bones are seriously deformed.

So, you admit defeat? smiles Dr Mariceau.

Yes, yes, yes, I cry. But I do not say a word. I want them to leave me, to leave me alone to the impossibility of my own deliverance. They claimed to be saviours, the doctors, but now the game is between them. I have had enough.

Enough. Enough.

No, no, says the older doctor smiling. I have every faith in the secret, though I could use the patient's co-operation. But he never asked for it. This too cannot be my fault. Everything is my fault. My wicked and punished body is at fault.

And the other rhythm, the darkest, most inward rhythm, lifts itself, swells, surfaces, which until now I did not notice because I have always lived with it. I thought that in labour it might go away. It does not go away. It is the rhythm of the Dwarf. The rhythm of the freak, of the monster, of the nightmare. It is the rhythm of the dreams and fears of all whose legs are straight, whose height is normal, whose shoulders carry their heads with floating poise.

The rhythm of the Dwarf is a hammer beat in the inmost cave where the Dwarf prowls for treasure in the dark. The Dwarf taps, taps, taps at the rock of security.

This is the time of the Dwarf. The Dwarf is malevolent and heavy. The Dwarf is the sullen weight. The Dwarf does not speak. It is no good asking the Dwarf to speak. The Dwarf does not like either words or silence. The Dwarf is the heavy weight of unspoken anger. The Dwarf goes down into the dark, stomp, stomp, stomp. The Dwarf lives in the dark so that they do not have to see the misshapen.

Oh yes, I thought in the great crashing waves of labour, in the sweetness of giddiness of the intolerable pain, that I could leave the Dwarf behind. For twenty-eight years I have been the Dwarf, I have been carrying the Dwarf. I am the Dwarf. I thought that pregnancy would move it, that the new life swelling the body differently, making it a new shape, was bringing me to a new place where I could be woman, mother, something, anything that was not Dwarf. But now my labia are spread back, cut into, torn apart and the doctor's deep claws are inside me, grasping, tugging, struggling. Ripping. Inside in the dark cave is the child that the Dwarf has stolen away and kept prisoner. All children are taught to fear the Dwarf and rightly, rightly. Once there was a little girl who did not know she was a Dwarf, that little girl was me. But I learned, I learned. I learned that I am Dwarf, to be showpiece or to be terror. In this new world there is no place for the Dwarf. No one wants the shadow, wants the dark magic that is as old as the caves in the hills where we delve. Eight years ago the last official dwarf at the court of France died. I went to his funeral. To say goodbye to a hope. We have descended now from gods and the holders of dark power, when the High Pharaoh would dance in our honour, imitating our bodies, singing our songs by the hot Nile. We are reduced to this bed of pure pain, where for profit and showmanship this man with large hands opens up my body and pulls and pulls until it is broken.

So this is the time of the Dwarf now. A heavy time where words must be hewn out. Words can float in silence like bubbles, joyful and coloured. But first they must be hewn out. Hacked painfully, heavily, out of the mine of noise which is the Dwarf's place. The Dwarf hates the baby inside me and will not let the baby be born. It is the Dwarf that has bent and deformed my pubic bones so that the baby cannot escape from the cave. The Dwarf hates all children, because once someone laughed, and in the laughter the Dwarf was born.

What I saw in his eyes was perhaps not there. After I knew he saw me as Dwarf and saw it salaciously. But for one sweet moment I saw only affection and desire. It seemed worth the risk, for a few hours not to be Dwarf but to be lover. That moment of escape, of hope, was signing my own death warrant and I knew it. He proffered death who proffered love, because there is no life for the deformed, no hope, no way out. When the roots go down, wriggling like a baby's toes, joyfully down into the warm wet earth, what happens when they hit the deep unmovable rock of the mountain of the Dwarf? They cannot go down or round. I know that now as I push and push and push on this baby, trying to push it down, push it through, push it out into the light, and I cannot. He cannot for all his large hands and bluff optimism. The Dwarf stomps on each little root of hope.

There is too much pain. There is too much pain. There are too many rhythms and they do not work together. They have walked me for three days and three nights. The pain has assaulted me for over forty hours. The claws of the clever English doctor have dragged at my flesh for three hours; for three hours the body that he cannot see because it is under the sheet has been cut and shamed and broken. And the twenty-year weight of the Dwarf, the twenty-year rhythm of the darkness. It is too much.

Finally I am defeated. I break the silence. I say, 'Please, leave me alone.'

They take me back to the Salle St-Joseph. I feel the colder air on my broken body. I feel the explosion inside and the child drown in my blood. The other rhythms go. Only the low chuckle of the Dwarf remains. The belly-laugh of the dark place where the freaks must go. Welcomes. Welcomes me home for ever.

Twins

'Sophie's pregnant,' Matthew says, lounging in the doorway of the kitchen.

Matthew doesn't lounge. And the bluntness of his statement had the effect of 'Sophie's knocked up' from someone else. I would have expected him to say she was 'with child'.

'Sorry,' he gestures apology, noting my shock; a truncated priestly gesture, a bestowal of absolution, though this is his confession, not mine. 'I wanted to tell you before anyone else did. And then, I don't have anyone else to tell.'

Matthew fell out with his family when he converted and then, adding insult to injury, became a priest, in rapid succession.

'Surely they'll come round now.' I frown in an effort to decide. A Jewish family will, I believe, accept the child, if not the father.

'Yes. But not till it's born. That's the protocol,' he says lighting a cigarette. 'In five years all that pain will be history.'

All which pain? Does he mean theirs, or his, or mine, or ours? He catches my eye.

'Sooner,' I say firmly. 'Much sooner. Unless you intend to go in for some sort of extended gestation period?'

He scratches his head. 'Spring,' he says diffidently.

'Of course, spring.'

I shouldn't have said that. He looks quizzical and irritated by my smugness. Our tolerance for each other's presence is reaching its limit, after twenty minutes.

'I'm sorry,' he says softly, not fooling me for a moment. 'I didn't mean to – spring it on you.' He stands up.

I'm meant to accept his embrace now, his blessing. To give him mine. I struggle with myself to make the act of acceptance. He watches the struggle, misunderstanding is an accomplishment of some magnitude. I can see his contribution to it clearly; my own is obscure to me. I accept that piece of ignorance, and find I have accepted the rest.

Our embrace is brief. There's a finality in this event that could otherwise have been accomplished only by a death. Matthew and I didn't marry, of course, fools that we were. We could have escaped a marriage. We made it much harder on ourselves by living in defiant sin. Sin *bonds*.

Even our childlessness was a bond. A child would have stood between us, brought us paradoxically closer. But we never got the wheels of paradox, by which relationships turn, in gear. We avoided it.

Religion, as usual, made the avoidance easy. Once we'd used religion to flee altogether, into convent and priesthood, respectively. Then we fled again, into the arms of the world and each other. Now our backs are up against the wall, literally and figuratively.

We remained childless by the simple expedient of contraceptive pills. I took them under mandate from my adolescent conscience. The Church forbade them. Therefore I swallowed them, religiously.

We never worked out that we lived on less in the shadow of that monolith by making our every choice a chance to rebel. The Pope controlled us like a Victorian father. We lived for him, relentlessly flaunting his laws.

'Well.' I free myself, and smile at him. 'Let me know when

it's born.'

'Of course.' Dismissed, he turns away, waves in the doorway, is gone.

Now I can get on with the reality of what's happened. But last things first: my mental photograph album is flipping, apparently self-propelled, reminding me of other, similar scenes in this kitchen, with my erstwhile lord. Both of them, rolled into one: Matthew.

'I'm not God,' he said soberly, near the end. 'That's what the trouble is.'

'Oh *no*,' I answered, and he was on his feet, apologizing as he was just now, misunderstanding as he did just now. That was the first time I let the misunderstanding lie. That was my moment of giving up, and my first taste of the cocktail of relief and guilt that attended giving up.

The 'Oh no' he took as a cry of anguished denial was simply a contradiction. He was god, that was the trouble. I'd failed with him for the same reason I'd failed with his illustrious predecessor: they were both male.

Oh, come on, he'd have had to reply. That's all accidental. Genetic with me, cultural with Him. You can transcend that.

Yes, I would have replied, I can. But not as often or as completely.

Instead, I comforted him. 'We're the same kind of monster, you and I,' I said. 'That's the trouble.'

He brightened at that. It made him feel less left out. Then I began to lose my concentration, as I began to lose it just now, and to feel queasy with guilt as a result. The same thing used to happen in the chapel.

Transcend! It's like trying to fly and rejoicing in the fact that your feet leave the ground for a few seconds per each hour of effort. You jump. That's all. That's the leap of faith I made, went on making for six years of religious life and eighteen months of living with Matt.

All the images are male. It may sound a small enough thing

compared to the wealth of the imagination, compared to the mystical resources through which one can apprehend a sexless being, or that sexless mode which each being contains in its essence. But we are human, after all, and we cling to images and words. The pronouns are male. The address is to Father. The idea is a man. No use decrying the narrowness of my thought, no use to shout that ideas are ideas, pure and simple, and that one the purest and simplest of all. It's a He. I am not a woman who can concentrate for long periods of time on a man.

For a time, while a nun, I tried to work on it from that angle. If I could correct my own sexism, I thought, I might get somewhere. After all, why should it bother me, that He was male? Given that we had a spiritual relationship, why need it even appear in my consciousness?

It appeared above all in that spiritual relationship. That was the hub of the problem. Unbeknown to me then, my problem was not sexual. I could make love with Matt till the cows came home. But once we sat down, or up, to talk, my concentration slipped after the first ten minutes; I was somewhere else. Anywhere else.

It's a problem of will, I told myself. Just will yourself to forget that one unimportant superimposed little facet of His (or his) (supreme) being: maleness. But how can you forget a maleness when it belongs to a him? Or a Him?

I forgot them instead. Him and him; God and Matthew, faded from me with scandalous ease. When God went I thought a human love would bring Him back, or at least replace Him. But it wasn't the invisible God I didn't believe in, it was the male one. I didn't believe in Matthew either, for all our orgiastic folderol on the rug in front of the fire.

Sex was the last magic. We'd exhausted all the rest. If only we'd known that magic wasn't a staircase to mount till you reached the top, that it was more like a carousel, and even more like what the carousel itself flattered by imitation: the world. That the world was its own magic. The first magic. If only we'd looked around, instead of gazing stiff-necked at the stars.

I was first aware of Sophie as a rival. The rivalry intrigued me. It was the grain of sand inside my shell that's since produced its pearl. Love, of course. The most real love I've ever felt in my life.

That's not saying much, some snide voice says inside me. Given your history, that's not much at all.

Maybe not, I answer calmly. But it's something. I'm grateful. At that the voice subsides. The word 'grateful' acts as a crucifix to such vampires.

I was intrigued because I couldn't imagine what she saw in Matthew that I was blind to. She saw him, I suppose. The one I missed. She was no theological sexist.

'Second-generation atheist,' Matthew said to me in description, when he first told me about her.

We sat over our drinks in silent, shared awe. One comes to long for a pure absence of God as one once longed for a palpable presence. That was the core of her attraction for me, as it was for him: her atheism. My reasons were different from his. I saw it as the one final way to shake off the shackles of Big Brother, truly to see the sun set on His empire, 'He' being all men, all gods, at least all within my memory and spiritual perception, as the hoary Earth Mother was not. A triumphant atheism would overthrow the patriarchy with one swoop, I felt, at least in my heart, where I needed it to be overthrown. Then I would be free to turn my attentions outwards, to love and to fight.

Slowly the means came to mind, never in so many words; this was one religion without paraphrase, one love without voice. It was all act, despite the appearances. I couldn't second-think it, or I'd have had myself committed, my head shrunk, my soul shriven. I began to live in an intense, daily relationship with Matthew's wife.

He made it easy for me. He dropped over to see how I was, often. I recognized that his visits were really an occasion to brag of his success. He'd made it, he was part of the human race. We'd sighed together so many times over Camus' dialogue between the two friends, one of whom wants to be a saint without God, the other of whom wants to be a human being, and its bald moral: that the second was the more ambitious. We harboured that same ambition, and we knew how far we were from achieving it.

We'd kept unfailing check on each other's lack of progress. For all our grunts and groans, we remained siblings, in fierce competition for our humanity, as if there were only enough for one. No wonder I'd committed a spiritual vandalism of his home, a moral theft of his bride.

'She's so open,' he'd brag. 'There's no duplicity in her.' He'd look at me, frankly gloating.

No wonder! Duplicity was our middle name, our family name, perhaps. Scruples bred duplicity. Moral strain bred duplicity. Confusion and fear bred duplicity. There wasn't an honest bone in either of our two bodies: but she was remaking him, from the marrow outwards, and I set her the task of remaking me.

I needed to love, and there were no more gods. Only a godless woman would do, and he presented me with one in the only guise I could accept her, and myself as her lover. Our story would belong to me alone. It was my insanity, in other eyes. I needed my insanity, finally. I had held it off long enough.

He showed me a picture. I wasn't so interested in her appearance as such. I checked the softness of the face, and the concomitant strength. All was as I had thought. I needed no more evidence.

He let details emerge unconsciously, as he prattled to me of their holidays, of the progress of the charity they ran together. She was a tireless worker, but she insisted on holidays. She loved the sea, and she took long walks alone.

Not quite alone. I accompanied her on those long walks alongside the waves. I trotted beside her, content with her presence, not imposing myself on her. I was a ghost, but an unobtrusive one. I understood how the dead must feel, in their hauntings. Respectful of the life they've lost, they take care not to impinge. I took care. I never attempted to violate her thoughts or her dreams. I only invited her, in ghostly form, into mine, and she graciously came.

My hand is trembling. What does this latest development mean, what does it harbinger for my love? I stand by the window and hear myself give the cry I stifled in Matt's presence. It would haunt him, and that mistakenly. What a waste of time, for him to suffer! Yet I could hardly wish this suffering on her.

No; it's mine, and mine alone. Because this is the point of severance. I'd often wondered how it might end. By death, I thought, conventionally. Maybe I'd blocked out the area of her sexual involvement with Matthew, involuntarily. Maybe. This possibility had never occurred to me.

I suddenly see its inevitability. This had to be the way of it. This had to be the end. Now that she's filled with a child, I must leave her. I must prise my thoughts, no, my prayers, loose from her, lest they in any way detract from her energy. I cannot even trust myself absolutely to pray a clean prayer for the child. I must turn my eyes away. But where to? Where can I go?

Spring. I've already intruded for some fourteen weeks of her term. I must relinquish all claim. Not that I've ever made a claim; and yet I have, abstract and unstatable. I must withdraw my love; but where to fix it? It will drive me mad if it stagnates, if it remains dammed up in me.

I have fought the good fight. I have broken faith. I have turned my mind from her at every conscious moment. If she sometimes steps into my dreams on her silent feet, I wake myself immediately and sternly, I turn on the light, I read her tread into nothingness. I erase her footsteps on the sands of my sleep, with salt tears.

I miss her desperately, then less so as I find I have a new preoccupation. I cannot account for it, I have not willed it, but I am beginning to experience many of the symptoms of pregnancy. I could have predicted this, but I have predicted nothing. The condition is not of my making. It is willed from elsewhere, that is, from centres of myself over which I can exert no conscious control. Indeed I believe I am undergoing this experience as a direct result of the control I am exercising in order to forget her. This phantom pregnancy has visited me in consolation for my loss. As such I cannot reject it, though I do my best not to court it or wallow in it. I observe it, I would once have said, it is part of creation and, as such, I wish it well. Later I would have said, part of whose creation? I have reverted to the first formula; the consequent question no longer troubles me. I know the answer, and it is not important.

The time draws close. I have dreamt of old friends, old acquaintances, people I haven't seen or thought of for decades. I believe expectant mothers often do so, as if to welcome the child into the dense circle of their friends and foes and into the denser circle of those who have escaped their love and their wrath, even their attention.

I am in pain. My waist bunches with waves. I know such manifestations are hysterical. I am not perturbed. This labour is real, according to the dwelling I have constructed in reality. If my house is built on sand, I shall discover it now. However that may be, I shall be changed, and for that I am, again, grateful.

The phone rings. It's Matthew.

'It's a boy,' he says laconically.

'Oh, yes.' I breathe out. My own ordeal is not quite over, but it is eased by this information as by an anaesthetic. Of course her child is a boy. I am having the girl. My thoughts are puzzled and puzzling; but they must be, at such a time. I sink down on the floor and writhe with the final wrenchings of my gut. What am I waiting for, I wonder, lying on my back looking up at the window, in the aftermath. What has it all been for? Am I going to die? I feel a definite sense of my own death within me, a certainty of it at this moment of – birth – ?

The question is a fleeting lapse of faith. Birth! Yes, I feel a certainty of death, not imminent but immanent. Never so sure before that I would die. Too gravid with eternity to live my time.

The apparent banality of my thoughts embarrasses me no more than it would any woman in this extemity. It has the force, moreover, of revelation, and the energy-giving authenticity of truth. It strikes me that I am not yet, as I thought, basking in a follow-up tranquillity. This is only the calm before the renewal of storm. With that thought comes another bout: and it is out; the voice boomed from the depths, the slip of paper cracked from the fortune cookie. I have dreamt often of my family, during these last weeks. My mild mother, my overbearing father. My siblings. My furtiveness among them, hiding my many resentments, my latent contempts and jealousies. I have dreamt them all, lately.

I squirm. Memory and pain are one. Something is leaving me with a slipper-smooth bound, a fish leaping slick rocks. The message forms into words. It reads, or speaks, or deciphers:

> You are still pregnant
> With the girl you were:
> Deliver her.

I nod.

THE FUNERAL STORIES

Requiem

The First Lesson
There was a time when you were not a slave, remember that.
You walked alone, full of laughter, you bathed bare bellied.
You say you have lost all recollection of it, remember. You
know how to avoid meeting a bear on the winter track. You
know the winter fear when you hear the wolves gathering.
You say there are no words to describe this time; you say it
does not exist. But remember. Make an effort to remember.
Or, failing that, invent.

The Second Lesson
In the late nineteenth and early twentieth centuries a quantum
leap occurred that shattered the comfortable assurances of
Newtonian 'truth'. It was the amazing synthesis of previously separate areas of thought/investigation. The sciences of
electricity and magnetism merged, with electro-magnetism
accounting for light, colour and radiant heat. Chemistry was
engulfed by atomic physics. Biologists uncovered electro-
chemical processes within living matter. The previously
independent 'powers of nature' were seen to be convertible
into one another. They were simply different forms of
energy.

Soon matter went the same way. All the elements of chemistry were found to be composed of the same building blocks in different combinations. Finally the building blocks themselves became nothing but particles of compressed energy.

Einstein's theories of relativity have shown that space and time are not absolute and that matter and energy are intimately connected. The velocity of light, 186,300 miles per second, dominates the whole Theory of Relativity and is the only constant in a universe in flux. On this constant depend all human standards of time/space. Light velocity is a constant, not because there is an absolute value in 186,300 miles per second, but because no material body (the mass of which increases with its velocity) can ever attain the speed of light.

Paralleling these ideas on a quantum level, people have shown that the presence of the observer and the instruments of investigation actually affect the behaviour of some sub-atomic particles. The objective oberver hence was added to the list of post-nuclear fatalities. The formerly basic ingredients of the atomic/material universe refuse bondage with the traditional either/or boundaries of dichotomous thought. They behave on some occasions as if they were particles, miniature lumps of matter, and on other occasions as though they were waves.

According to the Theory of Relativity, time and space are not only Not Absolutes, but are changed by gravitational fields. An interesting phenomenon is the Black Hole, where mass approaches the infinitely small and gravity approaches the infinitely large, from the point of view of the observer, and has the effect of sucking in everything around it, including light. If we were to take two identical rulers and could move one towards a Black Hole, it would actually stretch, become longer than its twin, relative to the observer. Space, then, expands in a strong gravitational field. If we were to observe two clocks, the one closer to the Black Hole would run slow, relative to the observer, compared to the one further away. Time slows down in a strong gravitational field.

The contemporary scientific revolution has effected the dissolution of one of the most extensive superstitious beliefs of the age: the materialistic, clockwork universe of nineteenth-century physics. But perhaps all of this need not be considered on the old true/false scale of dualities and polarities. Perhaps it can be used merely to suspend temporarily our disbeliefs.

The Eulogy
This is a story about four people. Three of them are African and one is northern European. Three of them are women and one is a man. Three of them come from the ruling educated élite of their time and one of them is a slave. Not the same three in any one case. All of them are Christians.

Their names are Felicity, Perpetua, Augustine and Sara. Perpetua was born in A.D. 181 and Felicity probably a few years earlier – they both died in Cathage in 203. Augustine was born in Algiers in 354, lived most of his life in university cities in Italy, and died back home in Africa in 430. Sara was born in London in 1950 and lives there now. But bear in mind, time is relative and slows down, relatively, in a strong gravitational field.

Vibia Perpetua is twenty-two years old. She is nursing her first baby. When he cries her breasts respond, magically, which is both satisfying and embarrassing. When she is away from him for more than a couple of hours her breasts grow hard and heavy, even painful. When she feeds him she feels a strange tingling as the milk lets down and she watches his eager greedy loving lips suckle and she is enchanted. She loves her son, ignores her husband, respects her mother and hates her father. She is beautiful, nobly born, highly articulate and very well educated. She is used to being admired and getting her own way; but despite this she is often frightened. When she is frightened she becomes more articulate than ever, protecting her fear – which she despises – with a brightness and a certainty which others find convincing. If you like her you say she has natural leadership potential. If you don't like her you say she is a bossy show-off. When she knows that the stage is set for her own martyrdom she thinks, rightly, that she is very young to die, but also, rightly, that she will look stunning in the arena.

Felicity is silent. Silent and sullen. Obstinate. There comes a point, she has come to believe, where words are impossible, where everyone else takes them over and leaves you none. There comes a point where only sullenness will pay. Where the sulking child has to take over from the grown woman. Where the grown woman has to lean on the mute strength of the sulking child who knows that They can yell at you, that They can beat you, that They can punish, even kill you, but They cannot make you consent, cannot make you smile, cannot make you obey. There comes a space, a time, when you just have to hunker down in grim sullenness, not answer back, not try to explain, not respond, just live in the immovable heavy power of your own silence. It will be enough, just, and it will be everything. Felicity is pregnant with a child she does not want. She has stepped outside the condition of her own slavery to proclaim her own freedom to believe in God in whom there will be neither slave nor free. It is an enormous effort laying claim to, new possibility. She has to burrow into the inside of her own silence and hug it there. There is nothing else.

Their story essentially is very simple. They are arrested with other catechumens – trainee Christians, receiving pre-baptismal instruction – during the persecution of Septimus Severus who had forbidden fresh conversions to this inconvenient faith. This makes the catechumens, but them alone, liable to the death penalty. They are arrested, imprisoned, baptized, tried, condemned. For three weeks they kneel back to back in the darkness while everything is taken away. Their children are taken away: Perpetua's by her doting family; Felicity's by a premature labour, painfully, publicly, totally endured. The one thing Perpetua truly loved, the one thing Felicity truly hated. There is nothing in the new space, except the dark. There is nothing left but their resistance of each other. No, no, they will not. They will not succumb. They kneel back to back in their desolation and will not move for each other. Here is their last claim, their last resistance, their last privilege. The privilege not to deal with each other, not to deal with the difference and the darkness and the hatred, that is in class and style and determination and desire. They resist. They refuse. Perpetua dreams her dreams and declares her visions. Heaven and hell are open to her and her companions receive her gifts with gratitude. She knows that Felicity will have no part in this; that Felicity walks her own silent road, not singing and dancing and performing, but battening down the hatches to endure, to endure and to endure. Felicity clings to her own secrecy; she knows that Perpetua is scared shitless, she knows that Perpetua clings to her dreams and her authority in order not to have to cling to her fear; and she hates her, she hates the brightness and the belovedness, she hates the ease of authority and the knowing. She clings to her silence in the dark and neither will comfort the other.

In the last night, in the last space before the dawn, something changes. It is their secret: who made the first move, who made the even harder gesture of accepting, affirming, responding to that move, I do not know. But in the morning they go out, shining bright and holding hands. They are singing, they are singing and their songs are an offence to the ogling crowd. They are women together and their hands are clasped round each other's in victory, not in peace – for there can be no peace between them – but in triumph, in exultation, in joy. They are not being led to the arena, they have no passivity; no, they march, they march as free women, and their fingers are entwined.

In the hour of perfect darkness there was a turning towards dawn, a turning towards each other from which everyone else is absent. There is a greed, a greed for death, a hunger that cannot otherwise be met. 'We came here willingly,' Perpetua says for both of them, declares it here in the middle of the arena while their post-partum, lactating, dripping women's bodies cause an unwelcome disturbance to all the audience. 'We came here willingly so that our liberty might not be obscured. For this cause we have dedicated our lives. This is our contract with you.' Our contract is that we are allowed to die. We have turned in the night, in a secret place, a woman's place together and now we declare that we have come here so that our freedom may not be obscured.

The animals are prepared for the killing: leopards and bears and boars; a mad cow especially for the women as is appropriate. The mad cow tosses them, but holding each other they help themselves to their feet. This is love, sing their battered bodies, this is a love that no one can take from us. Perpetua is so wrapped up in the content of her own ecstasy that she does not even notice the flesh torn by the cow's horn. Felicity smiles. Now they have come to the new place, Felicity thinks it funny that Perpetua should still be interested in ecstasy. In the end they are led, still singing, to the place of execution. They exchange a kiss. What is this kiss, this sweetness? It is called the kiss of peace, but there is no peace, only a wild eagerness. Their throats are cut. Felicity, stubborn to the last, consents to die. Perpetua, flamboyant to the last, insists on assisting her incompetent and pain-inflicting executioner with his job. She points, with elegant and manicured fingers, to the precise point in her neck where the axe-man should aim the blow. At the final moment she knows she cannot look on Felicity's severed head, at her still twitching decapitated trunk, so she has to talk. It is painful for the young man and she recognizes this without caring. Her last wish is that she is brave enough not to have to score points off a conscripted youth's social shame. And it is too late even for that.

Sweet sisters, tell me: what is this clarity? What is this eager embrace? Give me your sweet knowledge of death, give it to me, I beg them, and there is no answer; they have gone to a new place. In their new place there is orgasmic sweetness in dying. They live and love and die and do and be, as human people in a social world, that is changed and changed, transformed, re-membered, reinvented by the promise of resurrection and the recognition of presence. They are pierced to the heart and made alive with the consciousness of God, love of Christ, and power of choice. And in the moment of their turning, in the moment of their turning to each other when everything else was gone, when everything else had been taken away; then, there, at that moment, in that space, they became free women. Somewhere in that dark night their hands found each other, their lips found each other's and their crazed yearning for death and freedom found each other. I want what they have, and it is so strong that death has no more dominion but becomes but one more thing to be embraced . . . ah sweet lover when no other lover remained, the hymen broken in the ecstasy of love; the horns of the great cow an easy way through to hypostatic union and simple sisterhood. They bleed to death on the hot sand of the circus.

Now Augustine's story is more complicated, harder. Men's stories are, of course. Augustine is a man with strong sexual passions; for fifteen years he lives with his beloved, who is a whole strong woman, given the possibilities of her time; they have a son; for fifteen years he prays, 'Oh God make me chaste, but not yet.' But after his 'conversion' he leaves her, he never sees her again. He seeks not just to abandon the pleasures of his body but to break and remake his memory – so that what he knows he experienced as delight, he remakes as filth, reconstructs as repugnant to his longing self, renames as vile, as evil, as deathly. He declares that the woman and his own body have betrayed him: and therefore that he and his body are not the same thing. He is brilliant, educated, passionate and mystical. He cannot resolve his relationship with his mother. There is room for compassion. But there is no room for forgiveness; not yet. We cannot, Perpetua and Felicity and I, cannot afford it, not yet. Because he does not seek it. Because he does not know how much he needs our forgiveness and our benediction we cannot give it to him. And because he has hurt us; we live, past and future, recast in his model. Felicity and Sara and Perpetua and all are changed, transmuted, altered by his voice, by his observation of us, by his objectivity. He teaches, he teaches not alone, no not alone, but influentially, how not to see the free woman; and not seen she cannot exist, except in sweet dying, in dark turning, in useless and painful moments. He belongs in this story because he demands a relationship with Perpetua and Felicity and me. He crashes into the women's space with a mean generosity, and a vicious kindness. He preaches four sermons on their Feast Days and believes that he loves them with a holy devotion. Each time he names them, he names his own desires, that they should not be, that they should not be how they are. They must diminish themselves for him: that cannot be easily forgiven.

Look, times and spaces have changed in two hundred years; he, now Bishop of Hippo, returned home from the bright schools of logic and the power houses of Italy, can speak and his people must listen; they have no choice. He climbs into the pulpit, old and determined. No one risks martyrdom now. He looks on his flock and he preaches to us all:

These martyrs, dear brothers, were companions together. But above them all shineth out the name and merit of Perpetua and Felicity, the blessed handmaidens of God: for where the sex is the more frail, there is the crown more glorious.

[Frailty is relative: Saturninus, one of the companions of Carthage, was so shit-scared of bears, that they all prayed he could be despatched by a leopard, for his peace of mind and their honour. And so he was, and so he was.]

Truly towards these women a manly courage worked marvellously, when despite the pressures their womanly weakness failed not. Well it was for them that they were joined to one husband, even he to whom the Church is presented as a pure Virgin. Lucky, I say, that they clung to that husband from whom they drew strength to resist the devil – and how proper that women should cause the fall of that Enemy who through a woman originally caused men to fall. Yes, God allowed these women to die in a manly and faithful fashion . . . As for Felicity she was with child in her very dungeon; and in her labour witnessed to a woman's lot with a woman's cry. She suffered the pain of Eve, but she tasted the grace of Mary. A woman's debt was required of her, but she was succoured by him whom a Virgin bore.

Even as we heard their passion read and as tradition has taught us and as we know, these holy and valiant ones were not just of the female kind, they were Real Women. One was a mother, so that she had to cope with a natural love on top of the natural frailty of that sex. This was planned so that the Enemy might expect they would immediately yield. But they with the valiant and prudent strength of the inward man blunted all his devices and broke his assault.

In this company men were also martyrs; on the very same day courageous men suffered and conquered, but their names do not commend this feast to us. And this was so, not because women are to be preferred to men for their courage or deserts, but because the weakness of women made the vanquishing of the ancient Enemy more marvellous; and also because the strength of men struggled to win their own perpetual felicity.

Well, well. Which little remark brings me abruptly to Sara's story. This ought to be the easiest to tell, because I do not have to listen to other voices, do not have to deal justly with the other voices, with their time, their space, their social constraints, their social realities. Here I am. I can say what I want about me.

But it is not so easy. My entry into this story is through their text and my context. I know that. The connecting points are convoluted. I have to go into the maze with them; and it is dark in here. I first encountered their lives about six years ago; I was just starting to write a new sort of story – blood-strewn tales of madness and badness done to and by women in a timeless space between the boundary of myth and history. The texts of masochism these stories have been called: I do not know. I know that they came there, Perpetua and Felicity, and do not let me go. This is a story of an obsession. It is strange. I have wrestled with these two women ever since. I want to use them for my own morally uplifting purposes. They resist me. Their voices are clear and individual. They trouble me. I have long dialogues with them – though I have to write both parts and cannot pretend to write objectively. I speak mainly with Perpetua, because we are quite alike in some ways. But the dark growl of Felicity's silence; the screams of her dreadful labour; the inarticulacy of her slavery resound in the conversations. Both Perpetua and I often find this annoying, but we have to work on that.

Sometimes the conversations go like this:

SARA: I want to make a story about your life, about your courage and your death, your dreams, your madness and your love.

PERPETUA: I have already made that story. My life is my own.

SARA: But it's history. Women need to know it better.

PERPETUA: Retranslate my writing then, it is nearly unreadable.

SARA: But that's not my concern. Anyway, I'm not sure if my Latin is up to it.

PERPETUA: Oh well, if you're just a dialect-speaking northern gal. I thought you were educated.

SARA: Piss off. Also, though, I do have to say that your text gives me problems in itself. There are so many issues you don't even address. Like the question of class.

PERPETUA: The question of *what*?

SARA: Oh well, if you're just a liberal-minded educated imperialist.

[Felicity's growling noises tell us that this is silly. We wrangle and wrestle together. But basically friendly.]

SARA: Seriously. We'll leave that one out because of precapitalism and things like that. I do have a historical concept after all, the construction of ideology and all those ideas. But why, tell me why, in your wonderful, powerful dream, when you strip naked in the arena and wrestle with the giant Egyptian and bestride the air, and smite him with your heel and dance upon his fallen head. Why do you have to become a man to do it? Why? So intense and physical that dream, where your companions strip you down and oil your body for the combat; where they massage your breasts and cream the folds of stomach. Why do you have to be a man? Why do you have to deny your sex, to be strong? Why are all the women warriors men – you and Joan? You were surely strong enough in yourself. Why not do it as a woman? For us all?

PERPETUA: That was how the dream was. I wrote the dream as I dreamed it. You can't control a dream, you can't control a vision. It comes. It is not yours. And anyway you must remember, you must try to remember, that I'm a pre-Freudian. There are limits. I'm a pre-Newtonian too, as it happens, so don't come to me with causality and immutable universals.

SARA: I'm giving them up. I'm into relativity and quantum theory now.

PERPETUA: You can be into what you want. But I'm not fixing up my dreams to match your theory of feminism. I am who I am, that's definitive.

SARA: Yes, I can try to respect that. But, but there is one more thing and I hate you for it; one more thing that I do not understand. Why, when you wrote about so much, did you not write about Felicity's labour. When you could have told us, and you didn't. Why did you leave that to someone else? Were you jealous? Were you not interested?

There is a pause. 'This is a difficult question,' says Perpetua.

Finally she says: 'You must understand I hated her. I knew if I couldn't love her I couldn't die. But I hated her. And it was there, located in her pregnancy. Yes I was jealous, no I wasn't interested, but it wasn't that. Not that alone. Felicity has different ideas about motherhood from mine. I didn't think she had the right to take that risk with her baby's life. To pray for premature delivery, just so she could be with us. I thought her selfish. I had to learn. You see, I chose my son. But she, she didn't choose the baby. She was a slave, even your body is not your own, I could not understand that. She did not choose the baby, she did choose Christ, and death and us. It was her choice, and I couldn't bring myself to respect it. They don't send pregnant women to the arena: the Empire is very civilized, you know. I was proud of that. She was a slave; I could not understand, I could not. I didn't write about her labour, because in the end I couldn't write her story. I didn't want her to have it. Of course I was wrong. I was proved wrong when their prayers were granted, when they prayed for her labour and she went into labour. I didn't like it. It lay between us, heavy, weighted with our hatred, with our arrogance, with my ever more aggressive certainty. I tried to say we shouldn't do it. That we shouldn't pray that prayer. She thought I was dictating her life. We were on the dark side of each other. My baby had been taken away by my father. It was a place of pain for me. There is pain, there is difference.'

But sometimes when I ask her that question she gives different answers. And her central answer is always, 'Read the text, read the text, listen to my voice, hear me.' What is absent from the text, what I have to re-member, what I have to invent, that is harder.

Harder, but I want it. The sword is on her neck. She sings, rejoicing. She is gone to a place where I want to be; where I want to be and yet which I mistrust. I want her to answer, to tell me, to embrace me, enfold me, take me there, there to the gates of heaven and hell, there where the martyrs sing the victory song. So sweet, so easy, so tuneful, graceful, final. Ecstasy. Oh, sweet draining and the high spout of blood when the jugular is severed and fear is drowned in the red fountain, washed white in the blood of the lamb.

The Eucharist
They bleed to death on the hot, dry sand of the arena. They rejoice. The Church rejoices.

The Committal
The dialogue wavers, wavers and breaks up. It is nearly impossible. It is impossible to sustain. Our voices die away, battered by the differences of vision, of understanding, of

time and space, the different knowings, the different timings and spacings. And Felicity speaks at last: in an inaudible, wordless voice Felicity utters mutters which, caught on the frail vibrations of sounds that we desire not to hear because of our desire, her wordless silence says:

Freedom consists of voices that have been broken and blood that has been shed. Freedom tastes of pain.

The Interment

There is no objectivity, sing Perpetua and I in chorus. There is only the vision of possibility. We may not take each other's lives, each across time and space. We may not seek for heroines or theories for they are the same. We may say, here are good things, here are limitations, but there are more things in heaven and earth than we have ever dreamed of; and we explore the past, as we explore the future, for visions of possibility, for the expansion of consciousness, for the channels of hope.

Perpetua in her dream struggles up a bronze ladder; and it is hung with sharp and dangerous objects whose phallic symbolism I cannot avoid, even if she can. She tramples on the head of the dragon. Her vision of transformation glows in her copper-coloured face. Mine wavers in my pinkish one as I envy her the sweetness of conclusion; of finding the place so far into the dark that the turning becomes inevitable, forced into the arms of Felicity and death. Beyond choices, to the place where there is only purity of blood and death. But we both want, in the brave and singing mourning, we both want more possibility, the liberation into transformation and the power of a faith that makes a hearing space for our lives over the whole of time. We are different. The gap may not be closed. She is dead. I am alive. We are sisters.

The Blessing

Much of this is such an uncharted province that to ignore any maps and compasses which exist, however imperfect, would be feckless. My own suggestions as to how to begin are necessarily bounded by my own ignorance, the contours of my own history. The writings of other feminists, Marx's theories about history and class consciousness, anthropological studies of production in pre-capitalist societies, new work in social history which seeks to uncover everyday perceptions of the poor, demographic history, oral history. It is one thing to announce that all these could be useful. However, it is quite another thing to *use* them, and beyond my present knowledge. The writing of our history is not just an individual venture but a continuing social communication. Our history strengthens us in the present by connecting us with the lives of countless women. Threads and strands of long-lost experience weave into the present. In rediscovering the dimensions of female existence lost in the tangled half-memories of myth and dream, we are uncovering and articulating a cultural sense of what it *is* to be a woman in a world defined by man. We are tracing the boundaries of oppression and the practical assertion of self against their confines, the erosion and encirclement, the shifts and tremors of new forms of resistance. We are heaving ourselves into history, clumsy with the newness of creation, stubborn and persistent in pursuit of our lost selves, fortunate to be living in such transforming times.

The First Lesson is from Monique Wittig's *Les Guerillières; The Second Lesson* is based on an essay by Nancy Passmore in *The Politics of Women's Spirituality; The Blessing* is from Sheila Rowbottom's *Dreams and Dilemma.*

The Triangular Eye: 4

Once upon a time, I was the bride. Maybe there were lots of brides that day. But you don't think of that. I was the centre of attention. The centre of attraction. A magnet for all eyes.

I was not quite me. I missed myself in all that white, like a traveller lost in the snow. My reflection seemed to skate on the mirror's thin ice. I felt in danger. I could be the Snow Queen, with shards of broken mirror lodged everywhere, caking and choking the rivers of the veins, the seas of the arteries, till no feeeling moved along the nerves, till the synapses froze, till all was steel.

Then you two mistressminded my wedding. Hope you appreciate the liberated verb, Jane. You came and kidnapped me from that frozen fairy tale with its foregone conclusions, into another one for which there was no precedent, one we had to make up as we went along. I'd been an actress who'd clung to scripts, good at memorizing, hopeless at improvisation.

You changed that. As I sat, glad and sorry for myself, guilty in my relief, you were preparing the abduction of the play, Jane, the alternative direction of the standard wedding. The alternative direction of a standard life.

And you, Eve, waited in the wings to witness the event,

without knowing that you waited. You waited to capture the unique event, and you did. You got every important moment, all the unexpected expressions fitted suddenly as masks, matching Jane's mask, over the usual ones; or were they the masks? Every face was a question, against its will, and against the traditional, resolute setting. Faces and settings advanced the same argument, in spite of themselves. They argued that anything can change, at any time.

There were repercussions. Not only for us; Paul married one of my sisters, after the legal questions were settled, after our five minutes' marriage was annulled. Non-consummation. They consummated something, that very night, and were perhaps unable to play their lives quite as they might have, otherwise, afterwards. They were implicated. Paul had refused to remain my victim. They even invited us to the wedding, Jane, remember? We went. They did hire another photographer, though. I'm afraid people rather blamed you, Eve, as though you caused what you only recorded.

I said that to you at the time and you smiled, ruefully. I felt suddenly afraid. It was as though you agreed, as though you felt you made things happen, confirmed or concretized what was otherwise only chance, with your camera. There was some glimmer of humourless guilt in that rueful smile that chilled me. Could it be our Eve was a trifle touched, upstairs?

All artists are, you said, Jane, dear. She's developing a great technique. Leave her alone.

I said I'd no intention of handcuffing you. But I'd keep watch. And I felt Jane's theories of art were cruel to all concerned, but I kept that to myself. Our Jane was a trifle demented all along. None of it would've happened otherwise, would it, dear? So perhaps you were pleased to share the burden with innocent Evelyn, too pleased to reckon the consequences, quite.

So there we were. Two batty artistes and me. A good

supporting actress. The best. The part I played was the *enfant terrible* so that you two could cluck and forget your mad selves, from time to time. Your artistical woes.

It worked, ducks. I kept you halfway sane. Meanwhile, to be fair, you taught me a thing or two, such as how to let go without panic or violence. Such as how to hear my own ravings without shame or despair; how to listen. Once you made a tape of a drunken tirade, Jane, remember? Like this one, only I'm sober, now, though I'll take a sip at this juncture, from a glass drawn from our penultimate bottle.

I want a ba-by, I chanted on tape. I want a ba-by. It went on and on, and I couldn't help hearing, through my hangover, the voice behind the voice, like the ghost behind the waterfall, clear and separate and strange, stray evidence of other worlds, other ways. It sang behind the sobbing. It howled like a wolf behind the yelping puppy on the tape. It said: I want a mother. It said: I'm lonely, I'm afraid.

'If you really want a baby,' Jane said. 'Okay.'

I went on listening to that stranger's voice under the gush of the everyday as well on those voluptuous occasions when it poured forth like a geyser. I was trying to figure out what I did want, given that the ghost was there to stay. Given that the state of loneliness was the one and only state. But then the war came, and there wasn't time any more for such luxurious pursuits as figuring out how much unhappiness was endemic, how much spurious and curable. No time for belly-buttons probed like doorbells, no time for the stomach's thunder.

Life was all outside then. The world would need our help to be liveable, let alone bornable in. Birthable? By the time it was halfway there, it was too late for us. We'd worked too hard, we needed rest; and I was ill.

But what about you, Eve? With that fanatical gleam in your eye like your own flashbulbs? Your apparatus stuck like a hump to your back in that black bag you carried like a doctor's bag. I wondered if you felt responsible for *that* event, that bright flash that left all our eyesight impaired, whether we saw it or not. That we all saw, whether we saw it or not.

You worked with such steely, resolute will. You took pictures of outlying regions, like ours, first of all, pictures of the snowfall, of the freeze that came and killed livestock and plants. That wiped out our seasons, our time of day, our sleep. Our little exchanges, our conversations with the sun and the moon. We were isolated in the universe, as if we were diseased. We were.

You took pictures of it all. Most of us gladly closed our eyes when we could. You kept yours open as if with steel pins. We shared out our guilt. You kept yours to chew alone. We all suffered the cold almost gladly, like penitents. You allowed yourself no gladness, no absolution. Something happened to you. We all blamed ourselves for surviving. It was as if you blamed yourself for existing before the event, for existing at all. We all felt unclean, and yet you alone wore a bell that set you apart.

I didn't know till now what they'd lost, those who died. I knew they'd lost their lives. But I didn't know till now that they'd lost their deaths. It may sound like I'm making a virtue of necessity, but I want my death, which isn't to say that I want to die. They're two different things.

Yet I sit here blubbing like a big baby on my deathbed. Oh, mother! Receive me. I sent a foundling prayer to some imagined mother on my wedding day, and look at the answer I got! A lover in rubber-face mask and a roomful of rubbernecks, and a bouncing-ever-after rubber life.

On to the funeral. I want no kidnapping of my corpse. You're not to hijack the stiff like you hijacked the bride. It's my funeral. Or I'll make your lives a misery, I swear. Don't think I'll care. I'll ruin every photo you take, Evelyn, I'll draw moustaches on your every bride, I'll plant dogshit in stacks on your every landscape. They'll never believe it's accidental.

As for you, Jane, I'll jinx your productions till you can't work as a janitress in any theatre in England. Till you're driven to doing street theatre, one-woman shows in the rain holding an umbrella over your head like a tight-rope walker.

So, are you ready? First, the will.

I leave you each other.

Jane, you'd sit here and mope. I won't have my home turned mausoleum or monument. You're to sell it and squander the proceeds, or bury them under the compost, I don't care.

Eve, you can stop smiling that appalling appalled smile. I told you I was worried. You're too bound up with the mass, too far from the one. Come back. Rejoin the human race. Or is it your first membership?

I leave you both in good hands. You're old warhorses, sorry. I mean you won't get in each other's way. You'll work round each other till you meet up by accident in the kitchen. Old workaholics, old egomaniacs. I've loved you both, every damned day.

Maybe I should have written this out, spared you the sniffles and squeaks. But why? You're tough, you're troupers. And I'm an old ham.

Eve, take your medicine: Jane.

Jane, you just be as good a dose as you've been all these years to me. You've almost made a human being out of me; here's a new challenge.

Jane. Do as you're told. I want you to unearth that old gabardine raincoat you wore to my wedding. And the sticks – oh, we used them to anchor those rosebushes. Never mind. Just put a rose on either side of me. That'll be crutches enough.

I don't want the old crone's mask on, mind. Coals to Newcastle, don't you think? I want it on my chest. But I do want the coat on. I never did think dead people should be buried in nightgowns and shrouds and sheets. I always thought it should be coats, anoraks, wellies. Clothes for a crossing. Who'd wear a nightgown to set sail on an ocean? Or even to walk round the corner? I want to be dressed for my travels, thanks very much. If I don't know where I'm going till I get there, well, I never did.

Eve. Don't take pictures, you old vulture. You've taken enough dead people. Just deck the room, will you, with pictures you've taken all along. Give you all something to talk about. Starting with the wedding, mind.

I want an all-night wake, in the old way. Leave me in here on the bed and just invite whomever you want. Lots of wine. That reminds me, I need a sip. Can hardly lift the glass. Time to go! Almost.

Mother. My voice changes like an adolescent boy's, squeals and growls. There's a blurring and blending of me. Like Scotch. A distilling. Something I've hungered for without knowing. Myself. Without the my.

Where was I? Drink and talk and in the morning I won't be there. You'll see. You'll have talked me out, dissolved me on your tongues like the eucharist. You'll have me inside you, tucked away. Inside you, where I want to be now one more one more

Jane!

The Triangular Eye: 5

You croaked.

Your voice, I mean. Before you – croaked. Your last call was a mating croak blunt as a bullfrog's. I came running. You grabbed me with someone else's strength and threw me on the bed.

Wet and slippery in your pond of sheets, my lady of the lake, white Frances, where were you? Close to a ghost those past weeks and then you rose like a pillar of cloud in your nightgown, a mountain of steam. Your breath came in scorching gusts. A storm in the dust bowl. You scratched me everywhere, cactus raking my neck and my breasts, the desert in bloom.

My bride. No! You were the crone, I the bride. We'd come full circle. You rose dancing on coals. Supernatural, my demon lover. All I had tried to be, you suddenly were.

I wanted to fight you, to fend you off. You'd be gone tomorrow, to another life. I felt a welling of resentment like that other time. You left me then, for another life, but I pulled you back from the brink, from beyond the brink. You were about to live happily ever after, wedged in dry ice. Your dress smoked like dry ice. I only saw you in your eyes. Preserved in aspic.

But I couldn't pull you back in your smoking nightgown, not by hook or by crook like a bad vaudevillian grabbed from the stage. I can't spirit you away this time, I'm outspooked, there isn't a hook or a crook that long or that curved in this world, not one that can duel with the scythe.

Nor do you want me to try. I know that this time just as I knew the opposite, that other time.

So why force me to savour what I'm losing? Good to the last drop, is that your ghoulish reply? My screams fall on deaf ears; oh, no, they don't. You listen with delight, you sadistic archangel. A messenger come to announce the measure of my loss, the scale of my disaster.

You smile.

'That's only the first little wave,' you wink. 'We used to call them appetizers, the first few, remember? The first few? Canapés?'

'Why make me remember?'

'Remember with me,' you say, wisely. 'It'll make it easier after. Don't save it all till you're alone.'

I'd thought you selfish. And you were making yourself remember, with me, for me, as you were relinquishing even that most painfully pleasurable faculty of all. Memory.

I groan. Oh please, don't be *good*! You're a baby at my nipple, only I'm the baby here, the orphan. The bride about to be widowed. You're mother, crone and groom. We circle back, we circle back.

Pain and pleasure never so utterly combined. I can't trace the horizon between them. You smile as if you know. You don't want to talk.

I want you to talk to me. I torture you. I can't let your voice go. I lick the soles of your feet till you have to protest.

I move upwards, your baby emerged, but a breach, feet first to tear you. I turn around, jockeying head first. Head over heels we roll, both born, both dying.

Relaxed, again, separate. Hated relaxation. Into shells like cradles, like coffins.

'Hello,' you bring up the syllables from a well almost dry. I hold your head, pour wine down you. Your smile's a sickle, a fingernail moon.

I lean on your breasts and cry. You, too, leaning on mine. The four-backed beast with four streaming eyes. The dawn. We've slept. You have all this timed.

'Cigarette,' you order briskly, clicking your tongue with enjoyment over the word.

I light it.

'Wine,' you demand. 'Come on.'

No. No. No. I stare at you. This is as we've planned. The last bottle, the pills, and the vigil into daylight, full glare of the sun's last publicity. Last night was your last surprise.

'Now,' you hiss, and I'm gone for the bottle and corkscrew, following your direction. I see fear in your eyes. Don't fail me now, it says.

No. No. No.

Pop.

We lift our glasses to toast what we cannot name. Our years. Always with the proviso: till this us did part. Our life. Not a seamless robe. More a patchwork quilt, all stitched together by hand.

Our hands grapple, then hold. The first of the pills go down with an effort. Then the next handful. I must make sure it happens, we agreed that. I cannot sleep now.

'Tired?' I ask you.

You nod.

Your cigarette's stubbed out. I light another one, but it's sheer bravado, a fire to keep away the wild animals. I want only your hand. Another effort to swallow brings tears to your eyes. Then apologies I kiss away.

'Brave,' I whisper.

Wine. One more swallow. Then you can rest. Not so easy; nature resists, I think. Doesn't want this. Last act of will.

Over.

Hold your hand.

Touch my head to yours, like an animal's salute. Reverence for your life. For what I have known and not known. Some mystery comes on silent feet, fills the room. I looked for absence. Instead there are these footsteps padding our floorboards, as your breathing grows shallow, then hoarse. Almost cover my ears, but I can't. Traitorous.

Silence. Sweat like smelly dew. Other smells. Footsteps withdraw. A door slams somewhere. I sit in flood. Without a word in my head. My tongue coated with you.

No need to search for absence now. A trapdoor's opened in the floor, the world leaks through. Cold, cold, endless draught from now on. Never warm again.

I stand, mechanically. Cover you. Weave towards the phone in the hall as the first wave rips my belly. Appetizer. Canapé.

The Triangular Eye: 6

I'm hiding. Invisible, invincible. My shell, my darkroom. I know what they say, my clever friends. 'She's in the dark womb.' 'The dark tomb, you mean.' I won't come out, you'll never find me, I'll bathe in acid and turn into a skeleton, like the ones I photographed. Then you'll be sorry.

Who? What for?

As if you didn't know.

The room refuses me, refutes me. Won't be a hiding place. It spits me out into the light. I don't want to go. I'm not ready. It's not time. How dare you decide? Why can't I be the one? It's a crying shame.

Who says I've overstayed my welcome? The long dark that swathed me, that wound me round and round, is unwinding, leaving me naked. I don't want what's out there to touch me, to spoil me; light spoils and soils, light destroys. Darkness is safety and freedom and peace.

I'm being tipped like water from a pitcher, being poured out on the ground. I cling to the sides of my cavern, the slippery walls. Trying for a foothold, a fingergrip. I don't want. To be, to breathe. All my serviceable life, one long *non serviam* after all, refusing light?

No. Remember the cities of ash. The charred worlds where

153

I went with my camera to bring back non-platonic pictures; from the world to the cave. It was a mission my bones knew for theirs. They bore me there.

Two cities. One from each side. The order unimportant, matter of seconds, like twins. Tale of two cities. Everyone in the world knew someone in one of those cities, or both, knew someone who knew someone in one of those cities, or both. Many, many worlds ended.

Then came our snow, our great grandiose punishment, as if we'd been consigned to Dante's last circle of hell. We lived there cheerfully. Almost glad to suffer. Replanting, inventing. Pictures on pictures, different as snowflakes, and also the same. Busy. An object lesson, they said. But lessons are subjects, not objects. I took pictures of the subjects of the subject lesson. So it could be learned.

But as I took . . . did I grow away, grow objectified? Have I become what I set out to fight? Contaminated by it, in the end? Why is this single solitary death so impossible for me to face? Like a single solitary life?

This is the bride I fell in love with on her double wedding day. Then later with the two of them. They fuelled me. They were the we so I could be the I. Like parents. But it isn't like that even with parents.

I was so certain, if I could just widen my vision till it cracked and splattered and spilled, like a birth where the mother splits open, if I could do that, let it knock and batter down the door, I'd not be insulated, how could I? And yet it seems now I used vision as an excuse. Inexcusable. And now it seems I've hidden behind locked doors all along.

It's so thin and empty in here now. No tiger, no muse, no nothing. Was it all an illusion? All the times I sat here and saw – even after it happened. I never lost the scent. Or the tiger. The golden stranger.

But now it seems to me changed. My vision of the old woman painting the tiger who springs alive into her dream at the easel. Now it seems another story, the lady and the tiger. Or. The tiger. Instead of that harmony, that trust. It seems the old, cruel story. Of the young man in the arena with two doors to choose from. Behind one a beautiful lady, behind one the tiger. The cruel young barbarian princess, the one who decides. Will she let him live, to love the lady? Or will she watch him be torn to shreds by the tiger, and weep over the fragments?

But why do I think of that now, when Frances is dying?

Why do I think of that? Did I tender my own gift too jealously, such as it was?

Sight. We trust it too much. There are other senses. We neglect them. Cats see at night. I took that too literally. We created capsules of sense-deprivation, to reproduce the conditions of space. We learned things, but not the things we needed to know.

There was perfume in here, caffeine and petrol. Water and night. Voices. Songs from somewhere.

The phone. I pick up my bottle of Scotch on the way, take a slug. Realize, lifting the receiver, that I'm out. Without thinking, to answer the summons. Then it's all Jane's familiar voice grown strained and strange. Too close. I hold the receiver away from my ear.

It's no good. They're both beyond me now. As they were on the day of the wedding. Universalized as I've sought to be. Reversal of roles. Theirs the personal, mine the universal. Turned around. How could it be otherwise? I'm here in the chorus now.

Robot-like to the car, with the bottle of Scotch. She embraces me, is not surprised when I pull back. No one is surprised when I pull back.

'Sorry. I am –'

I pull forward. I force my head up out of the sandpit I've dug for it. We stand clasped, and then we go in to her.

Death. The smell. We work as a team, washing, changing

sheets. The doctor has been, she's been efficient, she knows why. That's what you have to bear in mind. If you forget what your efficiency's for, you turn machine. Nothing is easier.

I wondered, in the first city, first time. Could I brain myself with my camera, take a picture as I went out? Then shut the thoughts away and went to work.

We work slowly. Stumbling. With tears and soap and perfume and tears. When I had all those bodies I couldn't make them particular. I couldn't find one of them. Now I see them all, in this particular eye.

We listen to the tape. Twice.

She's right. I wear an appalled appalling smile. Broken my sound barrier. Made me growl. Got golden shadows moving in the grasses of my mind. I had lost the scent. Fallen into dreamless sleep at the easel. Turned my stripes into rank like a general's.

Dressed her. Extraordinary, that mask on her chest. Makes her face so soft-looking, just hatched from under it. So white. My fingers itch to take her picture. She's forbidden it. She knows it would be escape.

People come, we talk. No escape. I grit my teeth, my stomach growls and growls, I finally stroll to their kitchen, make food. Joined by Jane. Never alone! Serve the food, smile. Through my clenched teeth. Sometimes the tiger is found in the least likely places; a sign of contradiction. Never predictable.

I lie down by her for a while and then I leave her, asleep. She needs her time alone, that's why I go. Left to my own devices, I realize, outside, I'd stay. I'll be back tomorrow, and every day until she's ready to come to me, until I'm ready to receive her.

I hung the pictures for her. Then I had to see them staring at me. I don't think I ever really looked at my pictures before.

Home. Frances, the birds sound like you laughing. Playing

some childish game. Insisting:
  Who giveth this woman?
  I do.

Brilliance Books is a lesbian and gay press and welcomes manuscripts from lesbian and gay writers on all subjects.